Charlotte Vale isn't just a pretty debutante, like London society thinks she is. Behind her golden curls and blue eyes is a soul that craves adventure. She won't be happy living a sedate and safe life with some duke or earl like her friends will—she needs more. So when she is presented with the opportunity to take part in an under-cover mission for England, she jumps at the chance. Even better, it involves finding her father, who has been acting as a spy in France.

Anthony Graylocke takes his career in the Royal Navy seriously. The adventurous life of sailing the high seas suits him. There's plenty of time to settle down later with a demure, refined lady like his mother, but right now he enjoys the freedom and excitement that commanding his own ship offers. The last thing he wants to do is accompany and protect the offensive, disagreeable, and unladylike Charlotte Vale on an undercover mission to France. Too bad his orders state that he must do just that.

But when a startling secret that will shock the core of the Graylocke family is revealed, Charlotte and

Anthony must set their differences aside and work together in a race against time to stop a sinister plan that could destroy everything they hold dear.

CAPTIVATING THE CAPTAIN

SCANDALS AND SPIES BOOK 6

LEIGHANN DOBBS
HARMONY WILLIAMS

This is a work of fiction.

None of it is real. All names, places, and events are products of the author's imagination. Any resemblance to real names, places, or events are purely coincidental, and should not be construed as being real.

1

Midway between Britain and France
July 1807

"ARM YOURSELVES! AT THE READY!" THE BRITISH sea captain howled out orders over the roar of the wind. Rain lashed against the wood of the captain's quarters, where Charlotte Vale and her mother were residing during the crossing to France. The ship bucked, and the shouts outside the cabin rose to a crescendo as gunshots rang out.

Charlie's heart galloped as she searched for a weapon, any weapon. What was happening? Where was Mama? The closest thing she found to a weapon in the captain's quarters was a letter opener in the writing desk bolted to the floor.

Crack! The ship shuddered, knocking the breath out of Charlie's lungs. Her heart beat painfully against her ribcage. She palmed the makeshift weapon and skidded out onto the main deck.

Something had struck the mast, nearly severing it. The second mast leaned against the first, a chunk missing from the middle. She wondered if the ship was going to sink.

Cold rain stung her cheeks, matting her blond hair and throwing it across her eyes. She shoved the tangled strands back behind her ear. Her mouth gaped as she stared at the colossal ship alongside them. It had three masts, not the two that their ship had, and must have held at least a dozen more people —a dozen more French soldiers, if the flag waving from the tallest mast was any indication. Long planks hooked from the enemy ship onto theirs as soldiers armed with sabers and rifles boarded the British vessel.

No. We have to get off. Charlie battled a twinge of guilt at leaving the sailors to their own fate, but her and Mama's mission was more important. They had to reach the continent at all costs.

Where is Mama? She was huddled in the shadow of the broken mast, out of the way and looking fierce. She was armed, too, with a kitchen knife that looked far deadlier than the little letter opener in Charlie's hand.

Charlie slid on the wooden deck, which was slick with rain and sea spray, as she dashed to Mama. The ship pitched on the waves, and she nearly introduced herself face-first to the planks. She threw out her arms for balance and managed to navigate the rolling deck.

"Mama!" she shouted over the wind as she got close.

Her mother, in her midforties and still a beauty, her hair as blond as Charlie's with only a touch of gray that seemed to blend in with the pale color, looked over. She met Charlie halfway across the deck. They clutched each other's arms for balance. "We have to get off the ship!" Charlie shouted.

"We can't! The French will blow anyone who tries out of the water."

Charlie's heart pounded like an executioner's drum beat. *This isn't adventure.* She thrust the thought away. It didn't matter what she'd thought this journey would be like when she'd pledged to undertake it. Now she had to see it through.

"Then what? If we don't..." Charlie's throat closed. She couldn't finish the sentence.

If they didn't get to land, they would never find Papa. Charlie hadn't seen her father in years—in fact, until last year, she hadn't even known he was still alive. Not only was he not in the marked grave in London where the family had buried his coffin, but he was a Crown spy. And now, after alerting the network that he had vital information, he had disappeared. Although her brother-in-law, Tristan Graylocke, and his brothers believed her to be as motivated as they were to uncover the information Papa had disappeared with, Charlie had an ulterior motive. All she wanted was to see her father again.

One way or another, she was going to see that happen.

"Go below deck. Trust the navy men to handle this," Mama said.

Charlie balked. From the way they were being overrun, they needed all the help they could get if they had any hope of making it out of this scrape alive. Another gunshot rang out, making her flinch and duck.

"Go," Mama insisted. "Find the letter!"

They couldn't leave without it. Two British women in France would cause a stir that might get them imprisoned or worse, even with their cover story. After all, if anyone investigated the tale, they would find that Charlie didn't have a groom-to-be. Nor would she, not any time soon. She had a much more important reason for venturing into enemy territory.

And Lady Graylocke, her brother-in-law's mother and the woman who had been like a second mother to Charlie over the past year, had been kind enough to direct them to a friend in France. If the French found the letter of introduction that Lady Graylocke had entrusted to Mama when they left, not only would their lives be in jeopardy, but so would Madame Renault's.

Still, Charlie hesitated, not wanting to leave her mother alone on deck in the middle of the battle. "What about you?"

"I am trained for this. You are not! Go below deck, Charlie. Now!"

The urgency in Mama's voice and intensity of her gaze made Charlie take a step back instinctively. Another gunshot rang out, and she fought the urge to make herself smaller by curling into a ball. What if Mama got shot? She couldn't forgive herself it that happened because she hadn't gone below deck and Mama had been too distracted.

"Go!" Mama turned her back on Charlie.

Swallowing, Charlie turned and slipped toward the hatch leading to the hold below. The captain's quarters were tight, especially when both women shared the space. There hadn't been enough room to keep their valises with them.

The latch slipped from her trembling fingers as she fought to get the cold metal open. The trapdoor fought against the wind as she shoved it high enough to squeeze beneath it. The moment she released the door, it slammed back into place.

"Please let the latch not have sealed itself, too... " She didn't mean to stay down here, not while there was trouble above. But if she and Mama found a way to safely leave the ship, they needed that letter of introduction. Mme. Renault might be their only point of refuge once they reached France.

A thin light, dappled with shadows as footsteps crossed overhead, filtered through the grate in the ceiling of the hold. The rain wasn't heavy enough to warrant the captain calling to batten down the hatches, and it undoubtedly wasn't the first thing on his mind at the moment. Charlie searched for her valise in the hold among the jumble of crates, chests, and barrels. She found it wedged into a corner next to her mother's.

With the small key she kept on a chain around her neck, Charlie unlocked the lock on her mother's valise. She opened it and groped around until she found the hidden pocket with the letter as well as their orders from Lord Strickland, Commander of Spies.

Aha! She gripped the letters between her teeth as

she replaced the lock and stuffed the valise out of sight once more.

The hatch leading to the deck blew open with a crash. Charlie flinched. She stuffed the envelopes down her bodice, between her chemise and stays.

A man dropped into the hold, bypassing the ladder. Charlie whirled, letter opener at the ready as she shakily stood. She spread her feet wider than hips distance to compensate for the roll of the ship.

Charlie had never seen a French navy uniform up close, and if she had her druthers, she would rather not be able to describe it in so much detail. No doubt her closest friend, Lucy Graylocke-Douglass, would find the experience titillating. But adventure, to Charlie, meant seeing new places—not the lecherous grin of the French soldier who had cornered her in the hold.

Charlie buried her fear, mentally tying it into the tiniest knot she could manage, refusing to show it. Hefting her letter opener, she said in shaky French, "Leave this ship, or I'll see you thrown overboard."

Her threat sounded weak and watery. Especially when the soldier countered it by drawing his saber. *Hell and damnation, I've done nothing but make him angry!*

* * *

"TROUBLE AHEAD, SIR. TWENTY DEGREES starboard."

Captain Anthony Graylocke, or Gray as he was called by his friends, accepted the spyglass and aimed it in the direction indicated by his second-in-command, Lieutenant Lawrence Stills. Two vessels were locked in combat. One flew the Union Jack, and the other, the French flag.

"Ready yourselves! Man the guns! We've got an ally in distress."

One of the nearest sailors muttered to his friend, "I hope a damsel in distress, too."

Gray and his ship had been in and out of port all year, sailing up and down the English Channel on a mission to prevent any French ships from catching the mainland unawares. Even when stopped in port—usually Dover or Brighton—the crew weren't given much leave, if any. And they wouldn't be granted the time to chase a woman now, either. This was war.

The vessel looked to Anthony to be a small navy ship, the type used as a courier between larger vessels and built for speed. If not for the unlucky shot that had clipped the mast and rendered the ship dead in the water, it might have outrun the larger French barque with ease. The only crew aboard would be British soldiers.

Ignoring the flippant comment from his subordinate, Gray shouted to the helmsman at the wheel. "Turn us starboard, twenty degrees!" He searched the crew milling on the deck below until he found the midshipman he sought. "Cooper! When we get close, see that the men fire a warning shot. Let's see if we can scare these French vultures off."

"If not?" Stills asked, appearing at Gray's elbow. The shorter man was slight of build, his expression serious for once.

Gray grimaced. "We'll have to board."

The warning shot had no effect, and he couldn't fire a full volley at the French ship without risking doing more damage to their ally. His ship, the *King's Grace*, pulled alongside the "damsel in distress," as his crewman had put it. His riflemen knelt along the port side of the ship, picking their targets and firing at their commander's behest. As their comrades started to drop, the French soldiers scurried like the rats they were.

"Hold her steady, and drop the plank!"

His men obeyed, hooking the plank onto the friendly vessel so that Gray and a small group of his men could board. He checked his pistol then turned to his second-in-command. "Pull up the plank the moment I'm boarded, and come round to cut off their escape."

"Yes, Captain." Stills knew better than to protest Gray's boarding instead of the second-in-command. Although it put him, the captain, in jeopardy, Gray's blood sang with the danger. He wasn't the type to hide behind his ship and let his men do all the work. If there was adventure at his fingertips, he grabbed it.

Drawing his pistol, Gray followed the first wave of his men onto the friendly vessel and into the thick of the battle. Allies grappled with the enemy, too close together to shoot safely. Steel clanged as saber met saber. Men yelped as they were cut or grunted if caught by an unexpected fist. The French bolted for their ship, shooting blindly behind them to cover their retreat. Gray returned fire then stepped into the shadow of the quarterdeck to reload.

The shadow of the *King's Grace* loomed behind the French barque as it pulled alongside. Stills's voice rang as he directed the men to trim the sails and lower the plank. Gray and most of the men boarded the French vessel, cutting off the enemy's escape. Pinned between two forces, the Frenchmen dropped their weapons and surrendered.

"Check every nook and cranny," Gray bellowed. "I want every last cur rounded up and at our disposal."

As his men shouted acknowledgement, Gray turned toward the open door of the hold. Sounds of a struggle drifted from inside. A man cursed in French. A woman responded in the same language, albeit with a British accent, "It's no less than you deserve, you dog!"

A woman? Gray cursed under his breath. Pistol at the ready, he sheathed his dirk and dropped into the hold, gripping the lip of the entrance to slow his descent. He landed lightly just as the enemy soldier sliced into the back of the woman's hand. She hissed, dropping the letter opener she wielded and clutching her bleeding hand to her stomach. It left a red line on her pale-blue dress.

The French blackguard leveled his blade at her. "Up against the wall."

The beautiful woman's face contorted as she sneered. "Or you'll do what?" Her eyes shone with inner fire. Her expression might have cut glass.

The enemy pulled out his pistol and leveled it at the woman. Her pink cheeks paled, but she showed no other outward sign of being afraid. In fact, she glanced toward the letter opener on the ground, her damp blond hair falling across her face. If she leapt for it, the fiendish Frenchman might shoot. Simply the fact that he'd cornered the woman was proof that he had no morals.

Gray aimed his pistol and shot. The blackguard howled in pain and buckled forward. Drawing his dirk, Gray advanced on the enemy and planted his boot in the middle of the man's back. He rested the tip of his blade next to the open, bleeding wound in the soldier's shoulder, a silent warning. "Are you hurt, other than your hand?"

Her gaze snapping with anger, the young woman bent to snatch the letter opener off the floor with her uninjured hand. The tip was red with blood. "I'd be better if you hadn't come. I had him perfectly well in hand before you startled him."

The enemy hadn't bloody well noticed my arrival! "A fine way to treat the man who just saved your life," he snapped. The hum of the battle was soured by her demeanor. A beauty she might be on the outside, but she was savage underneath.

"I am not some weeping damsel in distress. I didn't ask for or need your help." Without another word—certainly no mention of the thanks he was due—she balled her skirt and stomped to the ladder leading out of the hold.

Gray gritted his teeth and tied his captive's hands

in front of him with perhaps a bit more force than was necessary.

He was certain he'd win this battle with the French, but the battle he saw coming with the woman, he wasn't nearly as confident about.

2

*S*he was back, her hand sporting a makeshift bandage that looked like it might have been created from a strip of her undergarments. Lace edged the bottom of the strip, and the white material looked sheer.

Gray ignored her as he supervised the transfer of the French prisoners from the allied vessel into the hold of their own. Stills awaited them, grinning with triumph as they were marched one by one over the narrow plank and toward him.

Meanwhile, the beautiful harridan dogged Gray's every step. "Captain, are you listening to me? You must take me to France at once! We haven't a second to lose."

He didn't deign to answer. Instead, he sought out the captain of this vessel, a gray-bearded man of good posture and an air of weathered command. Gray straightened his shoulders as he approached, trying to cultivate a similar air of authority—difficult to do with his chattering blond shadow.

"I'll be taking command of the barque," he told the other captain. "Would you care to abandon ship? I'll transport your crew to the nearest port to await reassignment." With the ship's mast all but severed, it wouldn't be able to sail on its own. At best, a larger ship might be spared to tow it back to port to be repaired. Ships were precious at this point in the war, so the admiral would likely opt to try to salvage the vessel.

"Thank you, Gray, but I won't abandon my ship to fall into the hands of these French monsters." The man called Gray by his nickname, used among friends and equals. They must have crossed paths at some point.

Unfortunately, Gray had a much smaller memory for faces and couldn't pair the captain's with a name. He pretended otherwise. "With the prisoners, I can't risk a mutiny by delaying my return to land. I must deliver the Frenchmen ashore with all due haste. I'll hail the first friendly vessel I come across to render its assistance, but if another French scout finds you first..." His voice trailed off. The ship and its crew would be defenseless.

The man's face hardened. "I understand. I'll ask for volunteers to remain with me. Anyone who would rather await another assignment ashore can leave with you." The captain's eyes flashed with something between greed and wariness. He and Gray both knew that the French barque would need a captain and crew. Although the ship had attacked the smaller vessel and not Gray's, the older captain had been outnumbered and outgunned.

Gray wasn't about to let him claim the new ship as his prize. Capturing and outfitting an enemy ship to serve in the Royal Navy was Lieutenant Stills's best chance at promotion. Gray might be young at only twenty-seven, but he was stubborn. He hadn't risen so high in the ranks of the Royal Navy by riding on his family's coattails. That French barque was his.

Stiffly, he said, "Your men are welcome to join me on the *King's Grace*." When he found an admiral at Brighton, he would present the ship along with his recommendation for Stills to take the command.

The other captain nodded, reluctant. "I'll put out the word to my men."

Gray relaxed. When he turned, the young woman stepped into his path, arms akimbo. "I hope your men enjoy France, because that's where you're taking me."

Whatever beauty products she slathered on her

skin must have leeched out her common sense, because commanding him was not going to work. He could see no possible reason for turning his back on his duty. He was an officer in the Royal Navy, and as such, he obeyed the directives of his superiors. In this case, that meant patrolling the English Channel, not ferrying around a waspish blond beauty on a whim. "I will not." He tried to step around her.

She blocked his path, crossing her arms, her jaw fixed in a mulish expression. "It is imperative that I get there."

"I'll deliver you to Brighton."

Given the look on her face, it seemed a good thing that she was no longer in possession of the letter opener, or she might have used it on him. "This is a matter of life and death, Captain—"

He cut her off. "Why are you so adamant that I risk my life and that of my crew in order to deliver you into enemy territory?"

Her expression turned pinched. Reluctantly, biting off her words, she answered, "I have to... attend my wedding."

He nearly laughed. She was engaged? His gaze dipped to her hand of its own accord, not that he found any evidence of her engagement ring. She must have hidden it while at sea.

Shaking his head, he repeated, "I'll deliver you to Brighton." And given the way she seemed determined to demand her way even though she hadn't expressed so much as a second of gratitude toward him, he wished the groom good bloody luck with her. Perhaps she was sailing to France because no one in Britain would have her.

He turned away, striding over the plank to join his second-in-command on board the barque. She scrambled after him. When she shrieked, his instincts kicked in. He whirled and caught her as she lost her footing on the slick, narrow board. Lifting her in his arms, he carried her the last step across and set her down aboard the barque.

Breathless, she batted a limp strand of her hair away from her face and tilted her neck back to meet his gaze. "Thank you."

That she thanked him for? She would have gotten wet, no more. If he hadn't intervened with that French soldier, she might have been killed. She was mad.

He turned away.

"Wait!" She hurried to catch up. "It's more important than it sounds."

"That you get married?"

She made a face. "That I find my way to France."

Why don't you take a dinghy and row yourself

there? He bit his tongue before he made the sugges-
tion. The young woman, oblivious to his irritation,
glared at him, as if by so doing she would be able to
change his mind. Not bloody likely.

He rounded on her, taking a breath to control his
reaction. If he'd dreamed of finding a woman stranded
on a vessel in the middle of the English Channel and
begging for his assistance, it would not have been her.

Perhaps this fictional woman would have looked
like her—for all her lack of common sense, the woman
was an uncommon beauty—but she would have been
more the sort of woman befitting his station. The sort
of woman his mother was.

Evelyn Graylocke, the former Duchess of
Tenwick, was a strong, polite, proper woman. She
didn't yield to the machinations of high society, but she
didn't resort to stubbornly haunting the steps of the
person from whom she wanted something. She
certainly wouldn't demand it as her due. Even as a
duchess, his mother would have asked politely and, if
refused, found another way.

The young woman glaring at him was absolutely
nothing like the demure sort of woman he hoped to
one day meet. This one was persistent, demanding,
impolite, and perhaps even a bit wild. When he
married...

It didn't matter. *He* was still a bit wild at heart and unwilling to relinquish his adventurous ways. Besides, she was off to France to marry her beau, and from what he could tell it would be a boon to all of England when she did.

Nevertheless, he gritted his teeth and tried to act in a way befitting his status and his family. "Perhaps we got off on the wrong foot. I am Captain Anthony Graylocke of the Royal Navy—"

The shocked look on her face stopped him midsentence.

"You're Anthony Graylocke?" She scrutinized him, recognition flashing in her eyes. "Of course. I should have known. 'Gray' is a nickname for 'Graylocke.'"

"Yes. As I was saying—"

She lunged for his hand, stopping his words again. Suddenly her whole demeanor had changed. His previous assumption was correct. The woman was mad. "I've heard so much about you!"

Oh dear.

"You look nothing at all like your brothers. The hair, I guess. All black. And maybe something in the eyes... "

Wonderful, she knew his brothers. That meant she was from a family in good enough standing to be invited to the same events as the Duke of Tenwick.

Somehow, he was certain his mother was going to hear about this, and he received enough letters from her, imploring him to give up his career and return home, as it was. He served his country proudly. That was the way it was going to stay, no matter the danger to himself.

Apparently, the biggest danger at sea was having his hands crushed. As the woman babbled, her words coming thicker and higher pitched, he gingerly extracted his hands. He flexed his fists as he returned them to his side.

What is she chattering on about? Still something about his brothers and performing his duty to his country? He did that already. He held up a hand, but she continued to talk over him.

"They would want you to help me. It's for the good of England."

That it was for the good of England that she married a Frenchman, he believed. He hoped it was a high-level military man. She might natter him to death and turn the tide of the war.

He cupped her shoulders in his palms, fighting the urge to shake her. "*Miss—*" Had she introduced herself during that torrent of words? "Forgive me, I didn't catch your name."

"Charlie. Charlotte, that is. Charlotte Vale."

His stomach sank as he recognized the name. "No relation to Frederica Vale, by chance?" His voice was weak.

She nodded. "Freddie is my sister. Though she's Frederica Graylocke now."

Miss Vale's sister was married to Gray's brother. Bloody hell, this was going to get back to his mother, after all. His temple throbbed as he tried to find a way to politely refuse her request without further riling her. He took a deep breath and dropped his hands. "Miss Vale—"

"Charlie."

"Beg pardon?"

"We're family. You may call me Charlie. Your brothers do."

He was not going to call her by her nickname. Their siblings might be married, but they had only just met. He straightened his jacket and said, "As beholden as I am to your family for giving my brother such wedded bliss, I'm afraid that I have orders direct from the Crown that are my duty and my pleasure to uphold. I cannot turn my back on them at a woman's request, not even one as connected to my family as you."

As he finished his calm, cogent explanation, she stared at him. Her eyelashes fluttered over her sky-blue eyes. After a moment, she muttered, "Nothing at all like your brothers. I guess you don't follow in their footsteps. Have you always been this stiff? If so, the navy is a good place for you."

Did she think before she spoke? He didn't deign to answer. "If you'll excuse me, Miss Vale."

He turned away to find Stills standing nearby, wearing an amused expression. It didn't help with Gray's sour mood.

"Wait!" She dashed into his path once more. Despite having traveled on a smaller ship more likely to be tossed around by the waves, she hadn't yet found her sea legs. She threw out her arms as she struggled to catch her balance.

Since she was in no danger of falling into the water this time around, he didn't help.

"You have to help me."

"Why is that?" he asked in a clipped voice. "Because of our connection? I have already explained that it does not supersede my duty to my country."

To his utter shock, she replied by sticking her hand down her bodice. Did she have no sense of propriety at all? He stepped closer to her, trying to use his body to shield her movements from the eyes of the other sailors.

Oblivious to the interested looks from the men,

Charlie produced two letters out of her dress. She examined each one before returning one to her bodice. "Here," she said, handing him the other letter.

It had just been down her bloody dress. "What is it?"

"It's a missive, signed by Lord Strickland, commissioning the ship of whomever I present it to. You must take me to France."

"Lord Strickland... the Commander of the Crown Spies?" He had been presented just such a paper once before, and it had been a pain in his bloody behind.

She beamed. "You do know of the network, then."

And so, it seemed, did she. *Bloody hell.*

Apparently her impending marriage was important enough for the Commander of Spies to take notice. Gray might have to ferry her to France, after all.

3

*C*harlie paced the length of the small captain's quarters of the *King's Grace*, shooting anxious glances at her mother. This room was as stiff and lacking in personality as the man it belonged to. The bed, the writing desk, and the chair were bolted to the ground. Nothing resided in the desk's drawers except paper, ink, and maps. The only evidence of personal belongings was a locked chest stuffed beneath the bed. By the time Charlie had finished one tour of the room, she had learned everything about Anthony Graylocke that there was to know.

She didn't know why his sister, Lucy, missed him so much. For although he was a captain in the Royal Navy, he didn't even have the loyalty to his country that the other Graylocke brothers did. If he had, he would have been taking her to France like she'd asked.

"You're going to wear out the floorboards," Mama warned, perched on the chair.

Charlie flounced to the bed and sat. It was as uncomfortable as the last bed she'd occupied. "We're going in the wrong direction. Why won't he listen to me? We're family, and he should trust me." Even if he didn't, she had a missive from Lord Strickland *demanding* that he trust her. He hadn't even looked at the page. He only tucked it in his pocket and told her to gather her belongings and bring them onto his ship if she was so adamant. Then he'd turned them north, not south.

"He will," Mama reassured. She didn't sound nearly as upset over the delay as Charlie.

Charlie wondered why, because Mama hadn't seen Papa in just as long as Charlie, although she had long known of his involvement in the spy network. The entire ruse had been concocted between them and the government so that Mama would be forced to beg sanctuary from Papa's nearest relative, Lord Harker. Charlie hadn't known that Harker had been a French spymaster until after he died shortly before Freddie's marriage, but Mama had. She'd been watching him for the Crown for years, while Freddie struggled to look after them and Charlie prepared for a coming-out she didn't want.

Mama added, "He has a duty to uphold, too. I'm certain that, as soon as he sees to that, he'll be free to render his assistance. If not, we'll find somebody else."

Charlie pulled her knees up to her chest and nibbled on her lower lip. "Aren't you worried we'll be too late?"

Turning in the chair, Mama reached out a hand and threaded her fingers through Charlie's. "Yes, I am," she confessed.

Charlie pulled away. "Then go out there—convince him to turn around!"

"I can't. If that directive from Lord Strickland hasn't convinced him, nothing short of a command from his superior will do so." Mama wrung her skirts, the only outward sign that she was just as impatient as Charlie. "Whether we reach the continent in two hours or ten, it makes little difference."

"Does it?" Charlie pressed her lips together. The mattress swung as she crawled to rest her back against the wall. "Papa's been missing for nearly two weeks. What will you do if we arrive only to find that we're two hours too late?"

Wrinkles formed in the corners of Mama's eyes. "That might happen no matter how quickly we cross. He disappeared with vital, sensitive information. We aren't the only people looking for him."

Charlie bit the inside of her cheek. "I don't care what he knows about Monsieur V or the plot that French monster put into place before Tristan shot him. I only want to see my father again."

If Morgan Graylocke, the Duke of Tenwick, had heard her say that, he might not have allowed her to accompany Mama. Mama had already been on edge about bringing Charlie along into the thick of danger, but Charlie hadn't been afraid to use every weapon in her arsenal. One of those weapons was the fact that she knew Mama was still an active spy, despite others in the family believing she had retired. Charlie had caught her leaving for meetings with persons unknown more than once, and she'd leveraged that to convince her mother that she was observant and keen enough to go with her. Charlie wanted to see Papa again—and if Mama couldn't stop her, one stubborn navy captain wasn't going to, either.

Mama sighed. "I know you do. I want to see him, too. But simply because we reach France doesn't mean we'll find him. This will take time."

"I know that. I've been practicing my French so I can search with you." Mama was much more fluent in the language than Charlie.

Mama's expression turned flat. "You shouldn't be so hasty to leap into danger."

"Why not? This is Papa... " Her father, the man she'd thought dead for years. If she'd been able to convince Morgan, Lord Strickland's second-in-command, to give her Papa's location before now, she might have gone racing off to the continent sooner. Freddie was still angry with their father for gambling and splitting up the family as a means to pay off all his debts, but Charlie had forgiven him the moment she'd learned Papa was still alive.

"I know it is." Mama sighed. "And I know you've a lust to see the world outside England, but your father wouldn't thank you for putting yourself in danger. It isn't nearly as glamorous as it sounds."

Charlie had discovered that an hour ago when the French soldier had cornered her in the hold. Her heart sped at the memory of his face. She would likely have nightmares tonight. But that didn't mean that she would let a little fear dissuade her from doing the right thing. "This is important—to us and to England."

Mama nodded. "I know. That is the only reason I'm here with you now. I know he's your father, but we have to think of him—and ourselves—as just another spy. The information he carries is what's important, to all of England. There would be no happy reunion for us if we didn't have a home to go back to."

"Surely whatever this Monsieur V has set up cannot be that dire."

Charlie hadn't been told a lot about the late French spymaster, only that the Crown had been trying to catch him for over a year and learn his secrets, but he'd been elusive. Even dead, he was considered to be a major threat to the country. Charlie couldn't fathom how. Surely he couldn't truly orchestrate a coup from the grave. He must have been bluffing.

For some reason, Lucy didn't think so. Whereas Morgan's information about Monsieur V had been sparse, Lucy had taken the time to tell Charlie a bit more about her misadventures only a couple of months back. It was thanks to Lucy that the former French spymaster had been captured at all, even if his captivity hadn't lasted long. Lucy seemed to think the man was capable of almost anything.

Judging by Mama's grim expression, she agreed. "It is dire, Charlie. No matter what the cost, we must discover what your father learned about the plot so we can stop it."

Charlie sat straighter. "Then we must turn around."

"Don't fret." Mama patted Charlie's hand. "This is only a delay. Captain Graylocke will help us. That letter we have from Lord Strickland ensures his cooperation. Once he thinks it over, he will realize that he has no choice."

4

Admiral Jermyn handed the missive back to Gray, his blue eyes hard. Although he had twenty or thirty years on Gray, the only sign of aging was a bit of white at his temples and the crow's feet around his eyes. "That is Lord Strickland's seal. The order is legitimate."

In the admiral's cramped dining room aboard the *Royal Justice*, Miss Vale preened next to Gray. The limited space meant she stood close enough to him that her shoulder brushed his arm every time she shifted. She had changed from her blue dress into a neatly pressed beige one and dressed her hair. They were presenting themselves to a navy admiral, not attending a ball. As before, her mother stood back, silently observing and seeming to fade into the woodwork.

Until this moment, Gray would have considered

the meeting to have gone well. He'd secured the French barque for his second-in-command, reported the location of the friendly ship in need of a mast repair, and secured the admiral's assurance that help would be sent. He'd expected to be sent back to his regular patrol.

Instead, he had to contend with a gloating woman next to him. She rearranged the curl next to her cheek and smiled. "Will Captain Graylocke be escorting me to France, or will you, sir?" She was brazen. Even Gray wouldn't talk to an admiral that way.

Admiral Jermyn didn't seem pleased. "Graylocke will do it. I'll see our new prisoners safely to land."

Hell and damnation. Gray tensed. "Permission to speak freely, sir?"

Miss Vale glared at him, as if she dared Gray to deny her request.

The admiral's expression hardened, but he nodded. "Permission granted." He sounded cautious.

Gray hesitated, choosing his words carefully. He ignored the glare leveled in his direction by the spirited young woman. Why was her wedding so important? Even if she was intimately connected to his family, he didn't see it as his duty to escort her. It was his duty to ensure that the French didn't invade England.

"Sir, it would be folly to take the *King's Grace* so

close to France. We're a large ship and easily recogniz-able. It could exacerbate tensions between us and start a battle we're stretched too thin to accommodate." He bit his tongue before he succumbed to the desire to tell the admiral what to do next. As much as he would love to request that Miss and Mrs. Vale be transferred to a messenger ship or even a civilian vessel headed for France, his training prevented it. He was speaking with a superior officer. He toed the line simply by expressing his opinion in such a matter-of-fact manner.

The admiral nodded. "Very well, then. Take the barque."

"I beg your pardon?" Gray's voice was weak. That was not his ship. He glanced to his left, where Stills stood with his back as straight as a pole. Gray couldn't tell a single one of the soon-to-be captain's thoughts from his impassive expression. He looked like a statue, as if he hadn't even heard.

Yet, it would be Stills's ship Gray would be taking command of, and he wondered what would come of the *King's Grace*.

Admiral Jermyn barked, "You heard me, Captain. You need to get to France unnoticed, and here we have a French ship newly fallen in our laps. A stroke of providence."

Once again, Gray glanced toward his former

second-in-command but found nothing approaching an ally in his expression. In fact, he stared straight ahead, over the admiral's left shoulder. Gray said, "What of the *King's Grace*, sir? I'm her captain. I can't fathom leaving her behind."

"*The King's Grace* will be returned to patrol. I need her as she was."

That was precisely why Gray didn't want to have to do this inane errand. Even if the Crown's Commander of Spies had given this mission his seal of approval, Gray didn't believe for a second that the spy network had a stake in Miss Vale's marriage. More likely, his mother or brother had spoken with the spymaster directly to ensure a personal favor. If she was a few days later than expected in reaching the continent, no harm would befall her.

Gray squared his shoulders and asked, "Under whose command, sir? Are you stripping me of command?"

"Far from it, Captain. Your ship and crew will await your return. I'll have my second-in-command, Wilson, transfer to the *King's Grace* temporarily, to oversee the crew. In fact, he'll ferry the French prisoners to Brighton. Can't have you taking them along, or you'd risk a mutiny."

Gray glanced at Stills again. This time, the man

seemed a bit agitated. It didn't show on his face, but the way he held himself was stiffer than usual.

Even though it might earn him a reprimand, Gray protested one last time. "What of Stills, sir? You've given him command of the barque."

"And he'll have it, after you see Mrs. Vale and her daughter safely to their destination. You're the senior officer here, Captain. You have command." Admiral Jermyn locked gazes with Gray. "See that it's done quickly. I don't want to have Lord Strickland breathing down my neck for unnecessary delays. Dismissed."

The admiral's voice was as clear a dismissal as his words. He would brook no further argument on the subject. Gray bowed, followed by Stills. Even Miss Vale curtsied, proving that she had some semblance of gentle manners hidden away. Gray held the door for the women to precede him to the deck.

The moment he shut the door behind him, he faced Stills. He clapped the other man on the shoulder. "Forgive me. I didn't mean for this to happen."

Stills smiled. "Think nothing of it, sir. It'll be as though nothing has changed."

His manner didn't seem sour or resentful, but Gray didn't see how he couldn't be. The man had just had a command dangled in front of him and then taken away again in the blink of an eye. And that wasn't to mention the fact that Gray had the challenge of commanding an unfamiliar ship that would be understaffed, with only a handful of the crew he was accustomed to commanding. The other men would be comprised of crew from the admiral's vessels.

Having said his piece, Gray steered himself toward the *King's Grace* to collect his trunk. He would need it on the other vessel, along with his navigation tools. The moment he stepped foot on his ship, he found himself cornered by the brazen Miss Vale.

She radiated smugness as she tipped her face up to his. "If you'd only trusted me, we wouldn't have had to waste so much of your time. I wouldn't lead you astray, Anthony."

Gray gritted his teeth and watched her walk away. He very much feared that she would lead him astray. For all her family connection to him, he didn't trust her at all. The odd feeling deep in the pit of his stomach told him she was much more than a pretty, innocent face.

5

*T*he French captain's quarters were more cluttered than Anthony's and therefore much more interesting. However, they were also smaller, so Charlie wouldn't be able to fit in the bed alongside her mother. She'd been given the second-in-command's quarters instead, with Anthony displacing the next-most-important officer on the ship. He hadn't seemed happy about his cramped accommodations. Frankly, Charlie didn't much care to spend more time in her allotted cabin than necessary, either. There was scarcely room in there to breathe, and not much more breathing space in the captain's quarters, where her mother would be staying.

In order to avoid brushing against one another while Charlie rooted through the French captain's belongings in search of anything thrilling or adventurous, Mama had to sit on the bed and keep her legs on the coverlet. They chatted while Charlie indulged her curiosity.

"You still have that letter?" Mama asked.

"Oh. Yes." Charlie straightened and tugged the missive from Lady Graylocke out of her bodice. She passed it to Mama for safekeeping.

"Good." Mama smoothed the page on her lap but didn't put it away for the time being. "We'll need this when we reach France."

Their destination was a small port town with a population of no more than five hundred. It was such an insignificant blip on the map that few remembered that it existed. Mama knew it to be a hotbed of smuggling activity between France and England. If Papa wanted to escape the country undetected, there was his best chance at doing so. However, the Duke of Tenwick had learned that French authorities were hunting in that area. Whether they hunted smugglers or Papa, Charlie didn't know. They had to get to the port quickly.

She sat on the bed next to Mama. "I don't see how Madame Renault is going to help. Aside from giving us shelter, I mean. She won't know where to look for a spy. Besides, we won't be able to confess our true reason for visiting France."

Instead, Charlie would have to pretend that she was getting married to a Frenchman she had never met. To those who knew her, it was laughable. If she were truly on her way to an altar, she would have to be carried on board kicking and screaming. She would sabotage the ship—and beg Anthony for his help getting *away* from France, not to it.

Charlie wanted new experiences. Even if it irked her to have to conceal her true purpose behind a ludicrous lie, at least she was finally getting the adventure she'd always dreamed about. She would see places outside England, the open sea air, a sleepy French port town. It was thrilling.

"You'll have to keep up the ruse when we reach France," Mama warned. "If Madame Renault cannot further our search, I'll need you to keep her distracted while I search."

Charlie bit her lip to stifle a sigh. Lady Graylocke, for all her generosity in recommending her friend and sending along a letter of introduction, couldn't possibly know the rigors of unearthing a spy who didn't want to be found.

Morgan, Lady Graylocke's son, had insisted his mother be kept in the dark as to the true nature of their expedition. Lady Graylocke knew Charlie well enough by now to realize that an arranged marriage was a sham of an excuse, so Mama had taken Lady Graylocke aside and explained some of the situation but not all of it. Charlie's father was not dead, as was presumed, but alive, and now that they believed him to be in France, they had to find him. To Charlie's astonishment, Lady Graylocke had made less of a fuss over Charlie accompanying her mother than Mama had. She'd simply given them the letter and instructions to present themselves to Madame Renault so she might ease their way. Charlie shouldn't have been surprised, though, because Lady Graylocke was a gracious, accommodating, and generous person. She was a good friend to Charlie and her mother and would help in any way she could.

But Lady Graylocke was a former duchess. What good would a peer do in this situation? Unfortunately, Mama was right. Most likely, Charlie would have to act the pliant fiancée while Mama claimed all the adventure and searched for Papa.

Charlie took a deep breath. As long as he was found, did it matter which of them did the deed? "Once we reach land, will we go there directly?"

Mama answered calmly. "I believe that will be best. We aren't locals, so if the town is as small as I am led to believe, even if we speak perfect French, we will be remarked upon." She raised her eyebrows at her daughter. "You do not speak perfect French."

Charlie grimaced. "I studied before we left." It had been years since she'd been taught the language, and most of the vocabulary had slipped from her mind.

"And you should continue while we're aboard the ship," Mama chided.

The last thing Charlie wanted to do was to be cooped up with a book while there was adventure to be had up on deck. The last crew with whom they had traveled had not treated Charlie's curiosity generously. She still didn't know much more about how a ship worked than which mast was called the mizzenmast, and since this new ship had more masts than the last, she couldn't even point that one out. Nevertheless, Charlie pretended that she intended to study more French as she slipped out of the captain's quarters. The open sea breeze called to her, and she never made it back to her cabin.

Didn't Mama understand? Excitement awaited beyond wooden walls, not inside them. It was adventure that Charlie hoped to find.

HELL AND DAMNATION, WHAT IS CHARLIE VALE

doing above deck? Gray gritted his teeth as he crossed the rolling floorboards, slick with sea spray. His body naturally adjusted to the ebb and flow of the waves—unlike Miss Vale, who appeared to be struggling to keep her balance even while standing still. She laughed and batted her eyelashes at Lieutenant Stills, who should have been overseeing the men—men who were almost certainly admiring Miss Vale's feminine form.

Although the rain had stopped for the moment, gusts of wind molded the dress to her body, showing every contour. The breeze teased out locks of her hair to tickle the column of her neck. Although she apparently had no sense of manners or propriety, she was lovely.

Gray couldn't speak for the men assigned to the barque from the admiral's ship, but if they were anything like the navy men he commanded, they were greedy for female companionship. If Miss Vale insinuated herself next to the wrong person at the wrong time, she might be in danger. If he was stuck escorting her to France, he would damn well ensure that she arrived safely. That meant none of this strolling unescorted above deck.

As he approached the woman and her companion, Stills, the lieutenant laughed. "It's hard to say what would fit her. I might call her the Veiled Smile. Unless you can think of a better alternative."

Miss Vale laughed prettily. "You flatter me."

"How do you know I am referring to you? Perhaps I've taken a shine to your mother."

The young woman laughed again. Her blue eyes sparkled in the gray light sifting from between the clouds. "Well played, Mr. Stills."

Lieutenant Stills.

He didn't correct her.

She tapped her index finger against her lips, drawing Gray's attention to them. Yes, his crew were animals starved for female company. Especially Gray.

"Why not a name that includes *luck* or *fortune?*" she suggested. "It was our good fortune that you happened upon us in time to save us, after all."

Gray gritted his teeth. So the maddening woman was willing to admit that she had, in fact, been saved by their timely arrival. However, she wasn't willing to admit her acknowledgement or gratitude to the man who had saved her—him.

"It was our pleasure, Miss Vale, I assure you."

Gray stormed up to the pair and cut the conversation short. "Miss Vale—"

She smiled up at him brightly. "Anthony! We were

just contemplating what Mr. Stills here intends to name his ship."

"Lieutenant Stills," Gray corrected between gritted teeth. "Soon to be Captain Stills, when I am no longer aboard the vessel. Address him with respect."

Miss Vale's eyes widened. She licked her lips, once again turning his attention to the shape of her mouth. She turned to the lieutenant. "Forgive me, M—Lieutenant Stills. I meant no disrespect."

Stills flashed her a smile. "Don't worry your head over it, Miss Vale. I took no offense."

Gray gripped her by the elbow and steered her toward the entrance to the deck below. She started to fight him but lost both her breath and her footing when the ship rolled due to another wave.

For a brief moment, Gray transferred his arm to her waist, holding her upright. Her body touched his intimately, reminding him of the pleasure to be found in holding a woman. He resisted. Releasing her the moment she regained her footing, he ushered her to the ladder leading below.

Although the captain's quarters abutted the deck, in order to reach those belonging to the officers, they had to climb down a ladder into the belly of the ship. The narrow corridor beneath the entrance was punctuated by the doorways to the various cabins, one of which Miss Vale should have been occupying at that very moment. Gray followed her down the ladder, clenching his jaw when she rounded on him at the bottom.

"Have you lost your way, Miss Vale?"

"Charlie," she snapped. "And no, I haven't. You just happen to be between me and where I'd like to go."

He clasped his hands behind him. "You aren't safe above deck. Please remain in your cabin, and I'll send for you the moment we come within view of France."

She narrowed her eyes at him. The light from above didn't penetrate far into the cramped corridor. Shadows swathed behind her, making it seem as though they were enveloped in darkness and privacy. The creaks of the ship and footsteps of the sailors seemed distant.

"I am perfectly safe," she told him. "Far be it from me to lounge in a stuffy cabin when I could be above!"

He took a deep, steadying breath. *You are addressing a lady. Act like it.* He clasped his hands hard. "I'm afraid you must remain in your cabin. That was not a request."

"Anthony..."

"I don't believe I gave you leave to call me by my Christian name."

She scowled. "We're practically brother and sister. You'll have to learn to live with it."

He stiffened. "I assure you, I do not think of you in a brotherly manner, and neither do the men above. The only thing running through their minds is how best to separate you from your drawers. Ask your fiancé, if you don't believe me. Men are the basest of animals, and men who have been separated from women for lengths of time are even worse."

Unimpressed by his warning, she crossed her arms. The movement pressed her skirt against her slim waist and emphasized the swell of her breasts.

Where he should certainly not be looking.

She didn't appear to notice his wandering gaze. "Don't think you can shock me, Anthony. And for the record, I have no fiancé to ask."

He frowned. "I beg your pardon?" She had explicitly bragged to him that she had one, the man she was set to marry.

Please, for the love of Jove, let the man she had her sights on know that she intended to marry him. Though it would be that fellow's problem if he doesn't. Not Gray's. The moment they landed in France, he was going to wash his hands of her. Battling a fleet of French ships was less of a headache than trying to deal with this woman and keep a civil tongue in his head.

She lowered her voice and leaned closer. "I'm not going to France to get married."

He had to have misheard. "You told me—"

"I know what I told you," she snapped. "That's the lie we're telling so no one guesses the truth."

The truth being that no one wants to marry her? Gray would have guessed that the moment they crossed paths. Now, atop being ungrateful for his assistance, she was confessing to have manipulated him into taking her someplace he didn't want to go.

"So I'm taking you to France on a lark?"

"No." She blinked rapidly, her thick eyelashes veiling her gaze for a moment. "Of course not. Don't be absurd."

Nothing about this situation was sensible.

"I need to go to France in order to find my father." Her eyes were big, her lips parted, and her voice no higher than a whisper.

He relaxed his pose, dropping his hands loosely at his sides. Why hadn't she told him this to begin with? If her father was missing—he must be, given the way she spoke of the matter—then he would have been much more amenable to lending his ship. He still would have needed to garner permission from his superiors, but he would have been much less of a prat about it. He took a deep breath. "Why didn't you tell me this sooner?"

"No one can know," she whispered back. She leaned forward, grasping his arm and squeezing.

He must be as bad as his men, because he couldn't stop thinking about the length of her fingers around his bicep.

She confessed, "If you weren't family, I wouldn't be telling you. My father is believed to be dead, and it is imperative that people continue to think so."

He frowned. "Why?"

"He's a Crown spy."

That explained Lord Strickland's involvement in the matter. "And he's gone missing from his post?"

She nodded. "Precisely."

Perhaps that was why she had been acting so waspish and unladylike; she worried for her father. He could understand that. Granted, most young ladies would worry at home, not gallivant into enemy territory. She didn't seem to realize the danger she was putting herself in. Did anyone else? "And Lord Strickland sent you to look for him."

Miss Vale nibbled on her lower lip. "Not exactly. I doubt he knows I'm involved. My mother volunteered to search—"

As Gray opened his mouth, she cut him off.

"Mama is a Crown spy, too."

Her family was riddled with them. Next, she would tell him that her sister, his brother's wife, was also involved in the spy business. He took a steadying breath. "Very well. Your secret is safe with me."

Relief blossomed across her face along with a winsome smile. "Thank you. I knew I could rely on you."

He held up his hand. With the movement of his arm, she released her hold on him. Without her touch, he felt strangely bereft. He'd been aboard ship too long. What he needed was a long shore leave to work free his frustrations. Perhaps once he delivered her to France, he would put in a request for one.

"I'll let you know when we reach France." He nodded toward the nearest cabin, assigned to her.

Her chin firmed. "I won't fall off the ship. I want to be above deck."

"No. I forbid it."

"You forbid it?" Outrage crossed her face, making her eyes glint with promise. It wasn't a promise any man likely wanted to have acted out upon him.

Gray held his ground. "Yes. I am the captain, and I forbid your presence on deck without an escort."

"You are not my guardian," she snapped. "You cannot tell me what to do."

He bristled. "I can, and I will."

A wisp of scent from her hair wafted to him. It smelled of citrus. How had she managed that? He likely smelled of sea and sweat. What little fresh water there was aboard a ship was kept for drinking.

Nevertheless, that delicate, feminine scent made him weak-kneed. It had been too long since he'd been at port. And longer, still, since he hadn't been forced to set an example for his men by restraining his extracurricular activities. He missed the way a woman smelled. He missed the way she felt against his body. The way Charlie would feel, if she lost her balance and fell into him.

He absolutely could not let her above deck. If his control was so thin, he didn't want to risk her safety with anyone else's. Even Stills. "The deck is no place for a lady."

She drew herself up. Her breath teased his collar, which he'd opened to take advantage of the cool sea air. "Don't tell me where my place is! I am a lady. If I am on deck, then that is precisely my place to be."

He clenched his fists at his sides. "It is your safety I am thinking about."

"Oh?" She cocked an eyebrow. "And what ill do you think will befall me if I should get some fresh air?"

"Men are animals, Charlie. Don't test me on this."

He knew precisely the thoughts going through the head of every man on this ship. He was afflicted by such thoughts, too, and he didn't even like her. It was the lure of her beauty, and nothing deeper. But even that could push a man who had been deprived for too long.

She laughed, as if the idea were ludicrous. Unfortunately, it wasn't.

"Do you have no faith in your gender? Every man on board has been a perfect gentleman."

"Until they catch you alone," he insisted. "Then you'll find the matter much changed."

"Is that so?" A smile teased at her lips. Such plump lips. They looked soft. "You've been alone with me for over five minutes. You haven't fallen on me like some kind of beast. Or are you going to tell me that you're a different caliber of man?"

He wasn't. He knew better than to lie. Instead, he cupped her jaw. Her hair, a bit tangled from the wind, was soft against his fingers. Her skin was even softer.

He was only doing this to prove his point, to scare her into compliance, or so he told himself. The moment his fingers met her skin, he lost his senses.

He pulled her up against him and kissed her until she lost hers, too. Her body fit against him intimately, a soft contrast to his hard physique. She gasped as her breasts were crushed against his chest. He took advantage of her parted lips and invaded with his tongue.

Push me away.

She didn't. Although hesitant at first, she soon tangled her fingers in his hair and met his every stroke. She tasted divine. He forgot himself, his hands wandering as he learned the shape of her, fitting her against him. Against his stiffening arousal.

Lawks! What was he doing? He released her with alacrity. She blinked up at him with owlish eyes, raising her hand to brush her swollen mouth. He swallowed hard and stepped back. "Go to your cabin and stay there."

He must have made his point, after all, because she shut herself away without argument. It should have been a victory, but it felt more like a mistake.

6

*D*ear Lord, the woman snores like thunder. The thin wall between Gray and Miss Vale proved little barrier to the sound. Bad enough their kiss continued to haunt him into the night, but now he had to contend with a constant reminder of her proximity. Her snores were louder than the waves lashing against the hull of the ship.

Charlie Vale was nothing like the woman he should be attracted to. If nothing else, her snores only served to prove that more. He tried to think of a more unladylike trait. Perhaps her stubbornness, or the impolite manner with which she demanded he serve her every whim.

Thanks to her, he was on an unfamiliar ship with a crew he didn't know, bound for a country that would have him hanged if he were apprehended there. Aside from what they scrounged from the quarters of the French officers and crew, he and his men had no disguise if they were intercepted. If a French vessel spotted him wearing his blue navy coat with the gold piping and buttons, their mission would be compromised no matter what vessel they sailed.

He was accustomed to sailing into dangerous situations, but he didn't usually have a lady aboard, let alone one so closely related to his family. His mother already thought him in hopeless peril. If any harm should befall the Vales under his watch, her opinion of his career would only plummet further.

Would Mother consider his kissing Miss Vale to be a form of harm? He did. He had a duty to set an example for his men, and kissing a woman under his protection was a violation of her trust. Never mind that Charlie had kissed him back with equal passion, her fingers in his hair, her tongue dancing with his. He hadn't conducted himself as befitting a gentleman, but she didn't act like a well-mannered lady.

She was brazen, outspoken, and demanding. Worse, when he'd kissed her, he'd stripped himself of all the qualities he'd like to think he possessed. Kissing her hadn't been proper. It hadn't been wise or honorable.

He had been no better than the animal he'd been

trying to convince her he was. How she drove him to such lengths beyond the manners to which he'd been bred, he didn't know. Well-mannered young ladies didn't tempt him to kiss them in the hold of a borrowed ship.

Charlie did.

He took a deep breath as he tried to purge the memory of her from his mind. It was the only way he could hope for any rest tonight. The howl of her snore next door made forgetting her impossible. Gray grimaced.

Come the morning, he would put as much distance between them as possible. He prayed that the wind would turn to his favor, so he might be rid of her all the sooner. No matter what, he couldn't lose his composure around her again.

CHARLIE HADN'T KISSED MANY MEN IN HER LIFE. The ones in the ballrooms and clubs of London were boring, vapid young fops who cared more for the way she looked than they cared for her opinion. They intended to live out their lives in the shadow of their parents, never taking a risk or stepping a toe out of line. Even hazarding a kiss with a man like that threatened to put her to sleep. There was nothing thrilling about it, nothing adventurous.

For all that he seemed as tightly buttoned as the men in London, Anthony Graylocke was different. He was an animal, or at least he kissed like one. He'd left her mouth burning and her body tingling from being pressed up against him.

And coward that she was, she'd hidden in her cabin. It wasn't that she was afraid he would take advantage of something she didn't care to give. No, Charlie feared that the moment he pressed his lips to hers, she would want to give him everything. Herself, her future, her chance for adventure. However chafing it was to remain in her cabin at all hours, she didn't trust herself not to provoke another kiss from Anthony if she saw him again.

Besides, she had a gift for Papa to work on. Even if the roll of the waves disrupted her stitches, making her redo more than she made, she had a coat for Papa that needed embroidering. Had she known she would soon see him, she would have started on it months ago.

However, by the time they reached France the following afternoon, Charlie had used up every last excuse to remain apart from Anthony. Especially considering that the stubborn man was for some unfathomable reason insisting upon rowing them ashore himself.

Charlie beseeched Mama with her gaze. *He has others to row us. Send one of them.* Unfortunately, if Mama noticed Charlie's unspoken plea, she didn't answer it. Charlie squared her shoulders. She would have to confront Anthony herself.

"Captain Graylocke." Charlie hardened her voice as she approached him. Seeing as he had made such a fuss about her mistake in addressing Lieutenant Stills, she didn't want to give him another opportunity to disparage her. She felt off balance in his presence as it was.

Anthony, standing in close proximity to Lieutenant Stills as they carried on a private conversation, fell silent and took a step back. His hazel eyes glinted like flecks of amber. He turned to Charlie.

"Miss Vale." His tone was clipped.

She met his gaze boldly, refusing to be daunted by his curt demeanor. "I hear you mean to accompany us to shore."

"I do."

Lieutenant Stills looked for a moment as though he meant to contribute. Anthony's glare silenced him, and she wondered what they had been speaking about.

Charlie clasped her hands in front of her middle

and resolved not to ask. "Thank you for your generous offer, but that won't be necessary."

Anthony raised an eyebrow. "No? Do you intend to swim ashore?"

She almost swayed toward him, intending to meet his hostility toe to toe, but the heat of his body seared her like a brand. She took a hasty step back, clenching her hands. This was precisely how their moment outside her cabin had gone awry. She bit her lip and took a deep breath.

His gaze dipped, lingering on her bodice and mouth before returning to her eyes once more. She gritted her teeth. He was just like every other man, ignoring her desires and opinions in favor of her beauty. But something about the way he caressed her mouth with his eyes made her battle the urge to lick her lips.

The last time he'd looked at her that way, he had pulled her flush against him and proven just how savage he was beneath his polite veneer. This time, they had witnesses. He wouldn't kiss her with her mother and half the crew idling nearby, would he?

"You need someone to see you safely ashore."

"You don't need to be that person."

Lieutenant Stills cut in. "My thoughts precisely,

Miss Vale. Sir, please allow me to row them to shore. You don't need to bother yourself with the matter."

Anthony's expression closed off. He showed no more emotion than a door. "Lieutenant Stills, I have given you a direct order on the matter. You may be in line to take command of this vessel, but I am in charge as of yet, and you will obey my command without question."

Charlie gaped at his sharp tone. Would Lieutenant Stills stand there and take the very public reprimand without question? The man's casual air dissipated. A twitch started in his jaw, but he bowed to Anthony. "As you desire, sir."

She didn't care if Anthony was the captain aboard the vessel, she wouldn't have stood to be spoken to in that manner. Charlie could barely stomach the sometimes veiled, cutting remarks of the *haute ton*. She supposed that she wasn't well suited to high-society life, nor to life at sea. Luckily, she hadn't been born a man, so the latter wasn't truly an option.

Still in a foul mood, Anthony divided his attention between Lieutenant Stills and her. "I accepted the duty of escorting Mrs. and Miss Vale to their destination. *I* will be the man to carry it out. Do you have anything further to say on the matter?"

"You're just as stubborn as your sister," Charlie snapped.

Anthony's face grew slack with shock at her pronouncement. She left him speechless as she approached the dinghy that would be lowered into the water and rowed to shore. If Anthony wanted to accompany them until the moment their feet touched the sand, it appeared there was little she could do to stop him. But she refused to let him have the last word.

Besides, he *was* just as stubborn as Lucy, in any case. She touched her hand to her mouth, wondering how she could possibly escape the memory of his kiss when he would be so close.

7

*G*ray's ill-fitting, borrowed French coat lay across his lap. His shirtsleeves were rolled up to his elbows as he rowed the two women ashore. Back and forth, back and forth. The swing of the oars and the ability to pummel the water with them in order to speed themselves along was a welcome respite from Miss Vale's glare.

Did she have a sweet, well-mannered bone in her body? She'd told him he, of all people, had Lucy's stubborn streak. He had three brothers, the eldest of whom was the most stubborn, self-important man he knew. Morgan always thought he knew what was best; in some ways, he was worse than Mother in inquiring after Gray's continued safety. But no, of all his siblings, Charlie chose to compare him to head-in-the-clouds, nose-in-a-book Lucy.

And she hadn't let up the comparison since they'd been lowered to sea, either.

"I don't know what Lucy sees in you to make you her favorite brother."

Apparently, she had lowered herself to bald insults now. He gritted his teeth and continued rowing, his muscles bulging. "What makes you think I'm her favorite brother?"

"She named her parrot after you."

"Lucy has a parrot?" Perhaps he ought to start paying more attention to the letters his sister sent. He'd read the one about her recent marriage. He'd never been fond of Brackley, but he'd settle it when he next returned home that the man knew to keep faithful to his wife.

Miss Vale batted a curl away from her cheek as she nodded. "A blue parrot named Antonia."

"Lucy named her *female* parrot after me?"

He didn't see how Miss Vale could possibly say he and Lucy were at all alike. She was his younger sister, and he was in turns annoyed with and fond of her. That was what younger siblings aimed to do.

Charlie looked smug as she answered, "She did. The bird says the foulest things, too."

Gray laughed. "Perhaps she was aptly named, then." He was a seaman, after all. He had learned a wide variety of colorful language that he refused to impart to his younger sister, whether or not it would help her with research for her book. "Did she ever finish that book she was writing?"

Her last letters told him that the princess heroine had changed to a pirate captain. That had been just before he'd been promoted to Captain and given a ship of his own; he hadn't been at liberty to answer her questions in the depth she had hoped. He wondered whether she'd ever found another navy man to provide the authenticity she'd wanted. Gray knew better than to believe that Morgan had given his permission for Lucy to take a venture out to sea.

"She did," Charlie informed him. "Last month, I believe. She still won't let me read it until she copies it out neatly, but it is done at last."

He made a mental note not to inquire after its status when he next returned home. Although he was willing to listen to Lucy rattle off her latest changes to the characters and plot, he didn't actually want to read the story. Books were much more Lucy's domain than his, hence why he found it so ludicrous to be compared to her.

After a moment, he murmured, "I'm happy she finally finished it." He left the conversation at that, thinking the tension between them assuaged until they reached shore. It would be no more than three or four more minutes, if he could keep up the pace.

Apparently, he'd underestimated Miss Vale's desire for confrontation. He scarcely halved the distance before she repeated, "I don't know what she sees in you at all."

He stifled a sigh. Clearly, she meant for him to ask her to elaborate. A wise man would ignore her. He'd already proven that he wasn't a wise man when he'd kissed her. Biting his tongue, he turned his attention to Mrs. Vale. Although she sat with perfect posture, like her daughter, her hands neatly folded in her lap, the older woman pretended to admire the ocean and shoreline. He would have thought her deaf if not for the amused tilt to her lips.

He rowed two more strokes before he bit off, "And why is that, Miss Vale?"

"Charlie," she corrected.

It seemed she hated formality. She continued to call him Anthony, despite the fact that he'd never invited her to do so. In fact, the only people who ever called him by his given name were related to him. He supposed, what with her sister's marriage to his brother, that she likely counted as family now. He tried not to picture what a family Christmas would be like if she were dogging his every step.

She informed him, "You're nothing more than a rigid navy captain."

He couldn't decide whether or not that was meant to be an insult. In his line of work, advancement was made based on one's manners and bearing as much as one's work ethic. His family name held a lot of weight, and when coupled with the polite demeanor expected of an officer in the Royal Navy, it had helped him go a long way.

He was fighting against his own instincts in order to do it, but he did the Graylocke name proud. Bit by bit, he was turning himself into the sort of man his father would have been proud of.

He didn't remember much of his father, the late duke, who had two sons older than Gray and one younger, who had a brilliant mind. Gray had always been a bit rambunctious, easy to rile and prone to jumping into situations without first considering the outcome. His eldest brother and youngest brother had received the bulk of their father's praise. Meanwhile, if the duke was taking time away from handling the estates, it was likely to deliver a reprimand to Gray.

Over the years, he'd learned to curb his hotheaded temper, as well as the wanderlust that prompted him to act first and regret later. The name Anthony Graylocke was no longer synonymous with misconduct.

Even if he sometimes chafed at the strictures of propriety, the itch for adventure was slowly dying down, year by year. By the time he reached thirty, he might even be staid enough to consider finding that demure, well-mannered wife. Perhaps by that time, the thought of living with her wouldn't put him to sleep.

With an ornery look, Charlie accused, "You have all that adventure at your fingertips, and you squander it! Imagine what some people could do in your position."

"Their job?" Gray grimaced and tried to gauge the distance to shore. Almost there. He wouldn't have to put up with her presence for much longer.

"You have a ship! You have the wide ocean."

"I have a responsibility to my country and the men assigned to me. You want a boat that doesn't come laden with responsibility, take this." He tapped the side of the dinghy with his boot.

The young woman made a face. "You don't appreciate what you have. You should embrace it."

"Embrace what?"

"The opportunity for adventure!"

He did. It was what had steered him to join the navy, as opposed to the infantry, when his father had passed on. He'd sailed across the Atlantic, chased down French traitors, and been in more battles and skirmishes than he could count. If that wasn't adventure, he didn't know what was. He countered, "I'll embrace the adventure of parting ways with you in France."

Charlie made a face. She looked about to start another argument, but her mother laid a restraining hand on her sleeve. Mrs. Vale looked from her daughter to Gray and back. "Let's remain civil, shall we?"

He would rather Miss Vale remain silent.

Fortunately, they reached the shore seconds later. He vaulted from the boat, sloshing through the shallow water as he hauled the dinghy safely ashore, where the tide wouldn't tug it off the beach. He then offered his assistance to Mrs. Vale first.

Her daughter attempted to disembark from the boat on her own. Her skirts impeded her progress. They tangled around her legs as she tried to climb out, and she lost her balance. Gray swiftly released Mrs. Vale's hand and caught Charlie.

She landed heavily against his chest, halfway on him and halfway still in the boat. He gripped her waist and lifted her out, depositing her on the sand in front of him. He battled the urge to pull her closer and released her instead, clearing his throat. "The town is west along that ridge." He pointed. "It shouldn't take us more than an hour to get there by foot."

"An hour?" Miss Vale echoed. "Why didn't we just dock in the harbor? It is a port town, isn't it? We have a French ship."

"It is, but we aren't French. It's safer to approach on foot." He collected the two small valises belonging to the Vales. Then he turned, striding toward the winding trail that led from the beach up the craggy cliff face to the top of the ridge. "Come, let's hurry. I'd like to be back on the barque by sundown."

Mrs. Vale picked up her skirts, squared her shoulders, and set out without complaint. Her daughter, on the other hand, was not so agreeable. She balked next to the dinghy as he turned away. He strode a couple steps on the soft sand, which was riddled with stones and wisps of seaweed, before the patter of her footsteps chased after him.

"You're coming with us? Don't be absurd. This isn't your mission!"

He took a deep breath. Her mother, already on the track ahead, didn't appear to hear Miss Vale's protests.

"It became my mission the second you thrust that missive from Lord Strickland in my face. If it is my duty to see you safely to your destination, I will see you to the doorstep of... " He frowned. Had either woman told him where in town they meant to go?

"Madame Renault," Miss Vale supplied. "She's a friend of your mother's. I have a letter of introduction here—" She reached into her bodice once more.

Gray looked away. "Keep it hidden. We aren't there yet."

She scoffed. "*We* don't have to go anywhere. You've delivered us safely to France. Mama and I can continue from here."

"I'm not going to leave two women in enemy territory without protection. That is final."

Charlie looked as though she meant to argue, but they reached the bottom of the path.

He stepped back and gestured for her to precede him. "Besides, if I wasn't here, who would carry your valises?"

Although she no longer argued his presence, she stepped back and crossed her arms. "I'm not walking in front of you so you can ogle my rear."

He bit the inside of his cheek to keep from laughing. "Very well. I'll go first, so you can ogle mine."

She scurried onto the path ahead of him. "I would never!"

Chuckling under his breath, he followed. Now that she'd drawn his attention to her figure, she did prove pleasing to look at. When she didn't have the breath to argue with him, at least.

GRAY FROWNED. "THIS IS THE ADDRESS?" HE spoke in stilted French, in case a neighbor happened to be listening.

Miss Vale tugged the envelope from her bodice and checked the address. "Yes," she answered in the same language.

With the day in full swing, everyone in the village had been too preoccupied with work to notice a gentleman escort two ladies into the town.

The harbor, a deep one if the three-masted ship in the dock was any indication, resided to the north. Squat, shabby little buildings ringed the water's edge, spreading out like ripples. The address on the letter coincided with a modest home on the southern edge of the town. It would have been easy for him to deliver the two women and continue on his way unnoticed.

If Madame Renault had been home, that was. Judging by the closed and weathered shudders and the air of stillness around the house, no one was in residence. When he stepped closer and tried to peek through the slats, the only thing he found was a layer of dust on the inside window ledge. Someone hadn't been home for quite some time.

Miss Vale rapped boldly on the door and waited.

"Don't hold your breath," he informed her. He strode around the side of the building to try looking through a different window. They were all latched from the inside, though one near the back had a corner broken off. He peered inside. Items were strewn across the parlor furniture. The bookshelf and mantel were bare. It seemed as though the occupant had left in a hurry, perhaps after a struggle.

"Are you looking for Madame Renault?" a woman asked from next door.

Gray stiffened. He turned, hoping that Miss Vale wouldn't answer in her questionable French, though his was no better. They would be discovered to be English at once.

And then? That three-masted ship likely belonged to the French navy. Merchants and couriers rarely sailed ships so big. If the enemy was in town, all three of them would be captured as prisoners of war. And if Mrs. Vale was unveiled as a spy... that future didn't bode well for anyone involved. Gray might be able to withstand torture, but Miss Vale, for all her brazenness, would not.

With a smile, Mrs. Vale tucked her hands

demurely in front of her and answered in flawless French. She spoke too rapidly and smoothly for him to understand every word, but he caught the words *south*, *friend*, *visit*, and *marriage*.

Miss Vale, who must have caught the last, did not look the happy bride. However, when the woman turned her attention toward her, Charlie brightened and pretended excitement with a smile. She almost fooled Gray, if not for the set of her shoulders. She would sooner do battle with the suitor who begged for her hand than marry him. Gray tried not to smile.

"And is this the groom?" the neighbor asked.

His heart skipped a beat. *Never.* He tried to smile, but it was strained.

"Brother-in-law," Mrs. Vale explained and then added something about her gratitude for his escorting them north.

Fortunately, the local woman appeared to believe the lie. She and Mrs. Vale spoke for a moment more before they parted, and Mrs. Vale beckoned for him and Charlie to follow. They strolled out of sight before the woman leaned close enough to whisper, "Madame Renault has not been seen for a week. She didn't tell her neighbors why she left—she simply absconded in the dead of night."

Perhaps her English ties had been discovered.

Whatever the case, they couldn't remain here. And without some form of shelter, the Vales would almost certainly be discovered by the authorities. He had to get them off the streets as soon as possible. "I know a family in town," he murmured.

"Friends?" Charlie looked dubious.

"I don't know if I'd go that far. They're smugglers to and from England."

Mrs. and Miss Vale exchanged a glance. "Are they trustworthy?" Mrs. Vale asked.

"That depends on who you ask. But they owe me a favor, and their residence is on the east side of town, near the harbor. If we can reach them, they will be able to shelter us. They might even be willing to help with your search."

Charlie didn't seem convinced, but her mother nodded. "It seems like our best chance. Lead on."

8

What if Anthony is wrong?

Charlie couldn't purge the question from her mind. Her ears roared as she crossed through town on Anthony's arm, as brazen as could be. She thought they should be hiding, skulking from shadow to shadow. Instead, he and Mama seemed bent on taking their time, each carrying a valise and strolling as if on an afternoon jaunt through Hyde Park. They carried on a low conversation as they walked, in French. Panic gripped Charlie the longer they walked like this. She spotted a French soldier down the street. Anthony didn't alter his pace.

Charlie struggled to focus on sorting out the translation to the conversation. She only understood snippets of Anthony's explanation of how he knew these people. They were smugglers whom he'd caught en route to England but hadn't prosecuted. He claimed that his enemies were French soldiers, not civilians.

That may be true, but she had to wonder what these French smugglers thought of him. They knew him for a British captain in the Royal Navy. If they decided to alert the authorities, Charlie would have no hope of finding Papa. She didn't want to contemplate what other ills would befall her.

As they entered the next street, out of sight of the French soldier, Anthony quickened his step. *He must be worried about being found out, as well.* Charlie matched his pace without complaint.

When they reached the house in question, he dropped his arm. "Stay behind me," he whispered. "And as tempting as it might be, let me do the talking."

Charlie glared at his broad shoulders as he rapped on the door.

After a moment, it opened to reveal a short woman nearing fifty, rounder on the bottom than on top. "Madame Estreux," Anthony greeted her in French, "may we come in?"

"Gray! What a surprise. Oh yes, of course, come in and rest your feet." She darted a glance up and down the street, wary, as she ushered them inside.

The moment the door was shut, they switched to English. Madame Estreux had an accent, but her vocabulary seemed much improved from Anthony's and Charlie's abilities. While the older woman greeted Anthony warmly and tried to extract information from him regarding their impromptu visit, Charlie sidled closer to Mama.

"What should we tell her? The same thing we were set to tell Madame Renault?"

Mama hesitated. "We prepared to stay with Madame Renault for days, perhaps longer than a week. We can't hazard staying with a stranger for that long."

"But what about Papa?" Charlie glanced at Anthony and the smuggler as he begged for shelter during the day, promising to leave come nightfall. However warmly the woman had greeted him, she seemed reluctant to offer him sanctuary.

Mama whispered, "We'll have to find him on our own, another way."

"I'll go out and search with you."

Mama shook her head. "No, Charlie. You're too conspicuous, and your French isn't what it might be. I've been trained for such a thing. I'll discover what I can, and if I catch wind of your father anywhere, we'll plan accordingly."

Warily, Charlie glanced at Madame Estreux and

Anthony, who now spoke more quietly. His back was turned to them, muffling the conversation further.

What are they whispering about? Charlie didn't speak the words out loud. She didn't know what her concerns were precisely, but she didn't trust the smuggler.

"Let me handle this," Mama said.

When she strode up to the whispering pair, they seemed to have reached some kind of truce. Charlie followed hesitantly as Mama spoke in fluent French. "Forgive the intrusion, Madame. We were set to stay with a friend, but it appears she no longer lives in this town. My daughter is an Englishwoman and speaks limited French like her father. Her father, the scoundrel, is on the run from the authorities, and we chased him here. He stole the money for my daughter's wedding when he left. Without it, her fiancé won't have her. I beg you, he must be here. We must find him before it is too late." She leaned closer, putting a hand on Madame Estreux's arm. "Do you have children? Wouldn't you go to any lengths for them?"

The smuggler nodded. She sighed. "I have a room in the cellar where she and Gray can wait for nightfall, but you cannot stay long."

Charlie had never realized that Mama was such an accomplished liar. She didn't know whether Anthony had alluded to some of the truth, but if he had, Mama's tale mirrored the truth closely enough in order for Madame Estreux to believe them. She even seemed a bit sympathetic, and she and Mama entered a tête-à-tête and spoke in low, rapid French.

Anthony glanced between Charlie and Mama, clearly curious, but he didn't interfere. In fact, he didn't even speak a word. He stood there with military posture and pretended to be a fixture of the foyer.

By the time Mama was done talking, Madame Estreux had promised the help of her family in looking for Charlie's father. She beckoned Charlie and Anthony closer. "Come, *mes amis*. I'll show you to the cellar. Once we've returned this evening, we'll let you out again. Does anyone need to use the chamber pot before you go in?"

Charlie did as Mama asked and didn't speak out of turn. She didn't draw attention to herself as she found herself shut in a cramped room behind the wall of the smuggler's cellar. As Madame Estreux shut the hidden door, closing Charlie and Anthony in together, Charlie held her breath.

If she wanted to find Papa, she didn't have a choice but to trust these people. Even so, she couldn't help but wonder if it would be Madame Estreux who next opened the door, or if it would be an enemy soldier.

* * *

MADAME ESTREUX'S HIDDEN STORAGE ROOM smelled of dust and stale air. The compartment, no more than two feet wide, ran the length of the room. Bottles of liquor and other smuggled goods lined the far end, packed in crates for easy travel. Gray and Miss Vale nestled hip-to-hip near the door, squashed together without space for him to stretch his legs unless he stood. It was bound to be a long afternoon.

He waited to the count of fifty before he used the tinderbox he'd been given to light a candle. Once the glow settled across them, he laid the candle atop the nearest crate. He tried not to think about Miss Vale— no, he might as well think of her as Charlie now, given their intimate accommodations. Eradicating her from his mind proved impossible when she was pressed so near to him.

They met each other's gazes. The memory of their kiss flared to life. He looked away and cleared his throat. "I don't," he said into the silence, his voice a bit hoarse.

"I beg your pardon?"

"Squander the opportunity for adventure." Her words from earlier, in the dinghy, haunted him. It was impossible that he had changed that much. If he had, it was for the better.

"No?" Charlie lifted her chin, her voice a bit breathless. "Tell me something you've done, then. A place you've been."

"I went to the Caribbean as a midshipman. We were chasing a small, fast cutter who had been dogging our ships. *The Ghost*, we called her, because she'd come up swift and silent in fog or early morning and hammer off a few gun rounds before we'd even see her to retaliate."

To his surprise, Charlie looked fascinated. She pulled her knees up to her chest and hugged them, leaning forward. "Were you ever under attack by this ghost?"

"She wasn't a real ghost, but a wood and metal ship. One of several the French were employing at the time, all identical and all made with the same design. Come in silently, shoot, and get out before the ship under attack could retaliate. The ship I was assigned to at the time, the *Frontrunner*, wasn't one of those under attack. We were assigned the capture or destruction of these ghost ships attacking us, along with a few others. We managed to corner most of them, but one of the enemy captains broke off and sailed fast for the Americas. The *Frontrunner* was one of our faster vessels at the time, and my captain thought we could catch them."

"Did you?" She laid her chin on her knee, still engrossed.

He'd had women fawn over him for his pedigree and his rank, but she seemed genuinely interested in the story. He grinned as he remembered the time. He'd been eighteen, still young and a bit brash, quick to run into danger.

"We did," he told her. "It took weeks of thinking we'd lost sight of them for good and then, on a calm day, finding them again on the horizon. When we reached the islands, we had to contend with other hazards—local authorities who didn't care for our interference and who might have been bribed by the French, pirates, unfamiliar waters with reefs and rocks we might run aground on. Finally, we cornered them between us and a reef, no place to turn, and came up upon them swift and silent like they'd done with our ships."

"What happened?"

"We boarded in the dead of night. The moon was full, giving us enough light that we didn't have to light a lamp. I was young then and supposed to stay aboard the ship to keep us ready to sail." He smirked. "It drove me mad to have to stay behind while the other officers got all the fun. But if I hadn't been on deck, we might have lost a lot of men. Amid the gunshots and clang of steel, everybody shouting... it was chaos. I was trying to keep an eye on the seamen still aboard, and monitor the fighting as well, when I noticed one of the lifeboats being lowered to sea. The captain was on board! I gave command to the other midshipman waiting with me and jumped off the ship, landing on the lifeboat to corner the captain. When faced with the mouth of my pistol, he decided to obey and ordered his crew to surrender to us. We came back heroes. I was punished along the way home for abandoning my post—given grunt work, mostly—but soon after I was promoted to mate, so I must have impressed someone with my act of bravery."

He'd told the story to women before. Most sighed or exclaimed over how he could have been killed! Charlie lifted an eyebrow. "You said this took place in the Caribbean?"

He nodded.

"Did you get to see any of the cities there?"

"We stopped for enough food and fresh water to last us until we returned home, but I had to stay on the ship."

She shook her head. "Then that's war. That's not adventure."

Caught off guard, he laughed. Had she just discounted the single most reckless act of bravery on his part as not adventurous? He didn't understand this woman at all. But for once, she wasn't accusing, so he played along and asked, "What constitutes adventure then, Miss Vale?"

"Charlie." She made a face. "Stop calling me that. We aren't in a ballroom. My sister is married to your brother. We're family."

Perhaps, in the loosest sense, they were. But he had never met her before in his life, and the thoughts conjured by her close proximity were not at all the familial kind. He licked his lips and repeated, "What constitutes adventure, Charlie?"

She beamed, her smile a bit smug to have him listen to her for once. Tucking her legs to one side, she leaned closer to him. "Adventure is seeing new places! You can't claim to have been to the Caribbean Isles, not truly, when you didn't step foot off the ship."

"We're locked in a smuggler's secret cellar. Is that what you consider adventure?"

Her expression fell. "It wasn't precisely what I envisioned when I came along—"

"Then why didn't you argue to go along with your mother?" He would have considered it daft, perhaps even foolhardy, but he had been surprised when she'd so willingly decided to hide away. The Charlie Vale with whom he was acquainted was far too brazen to hide.

Charlie pulled her knees to her chest once more. "We aren't here so I might see new cities and seek adventure. We're here to find Papa. If Mama thinks I might hinder that... " She made a face. "I should have studied my French harder. I'm not much of the studying type."

"Neither am I. Most of what I've learned, I've learned by doing, not by reading."

A smile pulled at her lips as she teased, "Apparently, not by seeing, either, if you're always confined to a ship."

His attention dropped to the curve of her mouth. Once more, the memory of kissing her surged. He licked his lips and leaned forward. They were utterly alone. Unlike the last time, when someone might have happened upon them, for the moment they had hours yet to while away in each other's company. That time would be much more pleasant if she were using it to kiss him instead of berate him. She'd come to life in his arms, further proving that she was no demure lady.

He shouldn't give in to his desire for her. He had more honor in him than to use her to slake his lust simply because he found her beautiful—at least, he did whenever she wasn't hounding him. Right now, with her lust for adventure still glimmering in her eyes and her lips slightly parted, common sense fled, and he leaned closer. Would her lips feel as soft as they looked?

He almost found out.

---

9

*W*ith Anthony Graylocke about to kiss her, Charlie's heart, already stirred from his tale of derring-do, skipped a beat. She licked her lips, trying to diminish the sudden tingle that rose in them. She didn't want it to interfere with the sensation of his mouth on hers.

In her mind, she was on a ship in the middle of the Caribbean, her pulse pounding from the new sights and smells and possibilities. She could only too easily imagine Anthony's tale ending differently, perhaps trapping them on a deserted island instead of being cooped up in this musty cellar. If they were stranded, with no hope of rescue, would she give in to the passion she'd found in his arms?

She leaned closer, hoping to meet him partway, but he stopped an inch from her mouth. He cleared his throat and pulled away. "Forgive me. It's... hot in here." He stood, stretching out his legs. As his shadow fell over her, Charlie recalled that they weren't trapped on a deserted island. They weren't even on a ship, let alone one bound for exotic new locations. They were stuffed into this cramped hideaway with no chance of adventure.

What was it about him that caused her to lose her senses? She'd been courted before—more than ever now that her sister had married into the Graylocke family. She'd always been able to resist them. A well-formed man didn't turn her head... challenge did. Perhaps that was what Anthony encapsulated. Kissing him was daring. It felt exotic. It made her body come alive and her senses more acute.

Clearly, he was able to resist her, unlike all those young fops constantly at her heels, yammering on about how her beauty gave them heart palpitations. What codswallop. Anthony hadn't tried to seduce her with flowery words or vows of undying admiration. Except for their one kiss, Anthony hadn't tried to seduce her at all.

He didn't now, either. In fact, he didn't so much as glance at her as he stretched. Had she been mistaken in thinking he wanted to kiss her? Perhaps he'd merely been shifting position and her eager response had scandalized him. She felt a fool.

Needing something to do to distract her from the scalding heat in her cheeks, she tugged the letter to Madame Renault out of her bodice. Since their contact in France had fled and they would be unable to deliver the letter, there could be no harm in her opening it to see what Lady Graylocke had wished to say. She slid her thumbnail beneath the seal, breaking it as she opened the envelope.

Angling the paper to catch more of the light as Anthony stretched out his arms, Charlie frowned. This letter wasn't written in English. It wasn't even written in French—she might have been able to read it, or at least enough of it to decipher the meaning of the letter. No, the jumble of script on the page didn't resemble any language that she knew. Her heart froze with the realization that it could be written in code.

No. Impossible. Lady Graylocke didn't even know about the British spy network, and Morgan had been adamant not to tell his mother too much about their true purpose in France. Perhaps someone had switched letters and replaced Lady Graylocke's original with this one.

Considering the letter had been inside her bodice for the better part of their journey, she doubted it could have happened then. Maybe before, when she thought it was locked in the trunk. But she wondered who... and why.

It seemed very unlikely, but perhaps this was some kind of shorthand that only duchesses or those connected to powerful families knew. Not for the first time since her dear friend had married, Charlie wished that Lucy were close by. She would have loved Lucy's advice right about now.

Perhaps she didn't have to wait to talk to Lucy. Anthony was also a Graylocke. He would know whether or not his mother was more involved in the spy network than she appeared. Charlie folded the letter and stood, dusting off her rump as she did. "Anthony—"

Her breath caught as he turned. The space in the hidden room was so narrow that his arm brushed against her as he did. Her breath hitched at their close proximity. *Kiss me.*

"Yes, Charlie?"

Accepting that she may have said that out loud, she licked her lips and tilted her face up just in case his answer had been an acquiescence.

Wait. What am I doing? She swallowed hard and stepped back, as much as the room allowed. Not far, indeed. She opened her mouth to ask about his mother, but footsteps caught her attention. "Do you hear something?"

He raised his finger to his lips to indicate for her to remain silent. She did, straining her ears.

Yes, definitely footsteps. Anthony heard them, too. He pushed up his shirtsleeves, his muscles bunching as if he intended to jump to violence if the wrong person opened the door.

The door swung open to reveal Madame Estreux, Mama, and a younger, thin man. Charlie quickly shoved the letter into her bodice again. "Did you find something?"

Mama nodded. "A man matching your father's description left on a ship bound for Portugal two days ago. If we have any hope of catching him, we must hurry."

10

*C*harlie's ears still rang from the news as she, Anthony, and Mama snuck out of the seaside town under the cover of twilight. Mama held Charlie's hand, Charlie held Anthony's, and both Mama and Anthony carried one of the valises. He insisted on leading, of course. They didn't dare light a lantern until they were away from the town.

Fortunately, the smugglers lived next to a cliff trail that led down to the water. The trail was hidden beneath overgrowth, but once Anthony found it, they soon whisked out of sight. In a port town like this one, comprised mostly of fishermen, anyone up after dark drew suspicion.

They walked for ten long, silent minutes before Anthony stopped to light the lantern. In those ten minutes, Charlie had more than enough time to brood, but none of her thoughts brought her comfort. Papa had pivotal information for Britain. He *should* be on his way home, not farther from it. She couldn't figure out why Papa would go to Portugal. Charlie had the deepest faith in Mama's abilities as a spy—after all, she had hidden her involvement in the spy network, not to mention the secret behind Papa's purported death, from her daughters for years. But what if, this time, Mama was wrong? Another man might have boarded a ship to Portugal, and Papa could still be in that town— or another.

The only thing Charlie wanted was to find Papa. The longer he remained in enemy territory, the more danger he was in.

As Anthony stopped to light the lantern, Mama brushed Charlie's elbow. "You've been quiet."

"I've been thinking."

"Whatever it is, it looks to be troubling you."

Charlie frowned at Mama. The light flared to life and cast a glow over Mama's face. Somehow, it seemed to magnify the worry lines etched around her mouth and forehead. "Are we doing the right thing?" Charlie asked. "Are you certain that the man heading to Portugal is Papa?"

"I can't be. Not until we catch the ship and discover for ourselves."

"What if it isn't? We'll waste time sailing in the wrong direction."

Mama rubbed her temple. "Nothing has gone according to plan thus far. We're lucky Captain Gray-locke is still with us. He could have left us on the beach, and we would be stranded in enemy territory. Let's take advantage of him while we can."

"And if we're wrong?"

Mama's lips thinned as she frowned. "Then we start again. I promise you, Charlie, we will not give up."

Charlie hadn't for a second considered giving up to be an option. She was going to find Papa no matter what. She only hoped they wouldn't be too late.

* * *

THE MOMENT THEY RETURNED TO THE SHIP WITH Anthony, Lieutenant Stills appeared at the railing. He cornered Anthony as the captain helped Mama out of the dinghy and back onto the ship. As Anthony accepted the valises from Mama and set them next to him, he said, "I hope you haven't moved our belongings yet, Lieutenant. We'll be playing host to Mrs. Vale and her daughter a bit longer."

Lieutenant Stills hefted the valises, one in each

hand, but didn't move. "I thought you were to escort them to town for Miss Vale's wedding."

Apparently, Anthony hadn't disclosed their true mission. He either distrusted his second-in-command, or he had simply deemed it unimportant, considering he had been ordered to bring them to port regardless.

Mama cut in smoothly. "The person with whom we were arranged to stay has left town."

"We're heading to Portugal," Anthony added, his voice tight as he lifted Charlie out of the dinghy. Her knees wobbled as her toes touched the deck, but she steadied herself against him. Once she caught her balance, he released her and turned to his second-in-command. "Weigh anchor at once. If we cut out to the open ocean and avoid the coast, we should be able to make good enough time to catch the Portuguese ship, even in a whale like this."

Lieutenant Stills would not be appeased by an order and followed at Anthony's heels, dogging him for more information as Anthony shouted orders to set sail. At this hour, most of the crew had to be roused from their beds. As those on deck scrambled to awaken their cohorts, Lieutenant Stills asked more detailed questions, prodding Anthony for information regarding their destination and why they were so eager to catch this Portugal-bound ship. Charlie wondered whether he would he confess what he knew about Papa.

She never found out. Mama, who didn't seem as concerned with the lieutenant's curiosity as Charlie was, led the way to the captain's quarters. Charlie followed. She set down the valise the moment they were inside. Mama, who had also taken the lit lantern, hung it from a hook beside the bed.

Charlie sat on the foot of the bed. "Assuming it is Papa on that ship, why would he have turned to Portugal?"

Mama joined her. She took Charlie's hand in hers. Charlie, needing comfort just as much as Mama, squeezed back.

"I wish I knew, Charlie. It could be that he was frightened to stay here too long. Perhaps the Portuguese ship was his only option out of France, and he was desperate. Perhaps he hopes to transfer to a ship bound for England once he gets there."

Too much relied on *perhaps*.

Mama clutched her daughter's hand and added, "We'll soon find out."

Charlie nodded. When she took a deep breath, trying to calm her whirlpool of thoughts, the letter to Madame Renault shifted against her breast. With the new problem in their quest to find Papa, she'd forgotten about the letter.

She fished it out of her bodice now. "I hope you don't mind, Mama, but I opened Lady Graylocke's letter to Madame Renault." Her cheeks flushed with shame. Mama had taught her never to open another person's mail, but she'd been curious.

Mama pursed her lips and arched an eyebrow. She said nothing, but her expression spoke volumes.

Charlie offered the letter. "It's written in code."

A flash of surprise crossed Mama's face before she hid it. After taking the letter, she carefully unfolded it and angled it toward the light.

"Can you decipher it?"

"I can," Mama confirmed. "Will you find the book in my valise and a pencil?"

If Lucy had been nearby, Charlie would have had both articles already thrust beneath her nose. She missed her dear friend, even if she was happy that Lucy had fallen in love. Or at the very least, she was happy that Lucy was happy. Ever since she'd moved in with the Graylockes, she'd constantly been in Lucy's company. She was more a sister than a friend.

But like Charlie's own sister, once Lucy had married, she had spent less time with Charlie. In fact, Lucy had moved out of the house. Charlie craved the company of her closest friend, even if she would never seek to spoil Lucy's happiness by confronting her over the loss.

Pushing aside thoughts of Lucy, Charlie quickly found the articles Mama requested and handed them over. She perched on the edge of the bed as she waited for Mama to decipher the letter. Lady Graylocke had told them it was a letter of introduction. However, if it was written in code, what did it truly say?

Mama finished and sat back. "It is a letter of introduction, as Lady Graylocke promised."

"That's all?" Charlie smothered a twinge of disappointment.

"I'm afraid so." Mama folded the letter and stuck it between the pages of the book. She tapped the cover with the pencil.

Charlie frowned. "But if that's all the letter says, why is it written in code? And how did Lady Graylocke even know to encode a letter?" This made no sense if there wasn't anything sensitive in a letter of introduction.

"I don't know."

"Are you sure this is actually from Lady Graylocke? Could someone else have substituted this for her original letter?"

Mama looked thoughtful. "She handed it to me

herself, but it was already sealed. I suppose someone could have switched them if she'd written it and left it on her writing table. In any event it has no big secrets. It's nothing to worry about."

Charlie's heart squeezed. Her mother might be acting like the letter was no big deal, but Charlie had other ideas. If someone had changed letters—and she was sure they must have—then they had plenty to worry about.

11

*D*ay after day, night after night, Gray found himself thinking about Charlie Vale. He couldn't get her out of his head. The way she wasn't afraid to speak her mind, even if her opinion conflicted with his. The curve of her lips and the way her body had felt pressed against his. Occupying the cabin next to hers didn't help. Her snoring kept him up half the night, and then he had nothing but his thoughts to keep him company. Even spending more time than usual on deck, looking over his men's shoulders as they did their work, wasn't helping. He was going mad. And it was all at the hands of one beautiful woman.

He had to get her off the ship and out of his life—the sooner, the better. With the anxious way his crew now conducted their work, peering over their shoulders as if watching for him, if he continued to breathe down their necks, he would have a mutiny on his hands. However, other than throwing himself into his work, he hadn't been able to find a way to distract himself from his attraction to Charlie.

She was a beautiful woman, no doubt about that, but she wasn't the woman for him. When he married, it would be to a soft-spoken, well-mannered woman befitting the son of a duke. And if he couldn't offer Charlie marriage, he certainly couldn't offer her anything less. His mother would skewer him, for one thing. Not to mention, he still had a duty to set a good example for his men. The Vales often came on deck when the weather was calm to stretch their legs, and he wouldn't let them suffer unwanted attentions.

Or even wanted attentions. When he and Charlie had been stuck together in the smugglers' cellar, he thought she'd tried to meet him halfway when he'd nearly kissed her. The notion that she wanted him as badly as he did her nearly proved his undoing. At all costs, he had to keep himself away from the temptation of touching her—a difficult thing to do when she took her meals in the officers' mess.

The only high point in throwing himself into his work was the speed he was able to excite his crew into creating. The barque plowed through the Atlantic Ocean. Although his flag officer had reported communicating with several other ships—including a Royal Navy vessel that had nearly run them down before being alerted of the barque's friendly allegiance—until now, they hadn't crossed paths with the Portuguese ship.

"There it is ahead, Captain!"

Gray bolted for the quarterdeck and the spyglass housed there. He turned it toward the ship on the horizon. It flew the Portuguese flag.

"Hail them," Gray commanded. "Tell them we request to board. I want to speak with their captain."

"Yes, sir!"

As the flag officer performed his task, Stills climbed up to the quarterdeck to stand next to Gray. "Is this the ship?"

"We'll soon find out." Gray put the spyglass back in its holder.

"Will you tell me now why we've been chasing this ship, sir?"

Gray hesitated. Having never been involved in a spy mission before, he didn't know how much he should disclose or to whom. However, Stills was his second-in-command. Gray would trust the man with his life. "A man aboard that ship has information for Lord Strickland. I don't know much more than that."

Stills frowned. "This man. He was supposed to be

in the town where Mrs. and Miss Vale asked to be delivered?"

"Yes."

"And this is connected in some way to her impending marriage?"

Gray didn't know how to answer that, considering there was no betrothal. However, he was saved the trouble when the flag officer called down, "They've agreed to meet with us. They're trimming the sails now."

Gray didn't have further time to talk, and neither did Stills. His second-in-command barked orders at the crew as they veered toward the friendly vessel. Gray retreated to the captain's quarters and knocked before entering.

Charlie, standing by the porthole and squinting to see out into the waves, turned the moment he entered. "Is this it? Have you found him?"

"We'll soon find out. Do you ladies trust me to question the captain in your absence?"

Charlie crossed to him, meeting him toe-to-toe. His body hummed with the desire to touch her. She wasn't terribly shorter than him, so he could kiss her without bending too far.

Unfortunately, they weren't alone. He clasped his hands behind him, holding himself in check.

Oblivious to the turn his thoughts had taken, Charlie met his gaze with fire in her eyes. "Absolutely not! We are coming with you."

* * *

Bringing Charlie Vale aboard a foreign vessel had been a bad idea, even if she had insisted.

"What do you mean, he isn't aboard your ship?" she asked.

Gray angled himself between her and the Portuguese captain.

The middle-aged man frowned as he tried to process her rapid English. Although the captains could communicate, the other man's English was rudimentary at best.

Charlie didn't appear to realize this. She continued her tirade, leaning to speak around Gray's shoulder. "What did you do to him? Did you kill him?"

Gray bit his tongue to keep from groaning at her lack of discretion. If she wanted to keep her secret safe, she wasn't doing a very good job of not drawing attention to herself. The Portuguese crew, for instance, stared at her with bald interest.

Fortunately, Mrs. Vale took her in hand. She laid her hand on Charlie's sleeve and spoke to her in a low murmur. Gray turned his attention to the Portuguese captain. He spoke slowly and enunciated carefully to avoid a misunderstanding. "Please forgive my colleague. The information we gathered suggests that the man we seek boarded your ship. Did you have a passenger fitting his description?"

The man nodded. He smoothed his beard idly with one hand. Charlie quieted and stiffened as the man answered in a thick accent. "Yes, we did. But we met with a French ship. He transferred to return to the continent."

"Back to France?" Mrs. Vale murmured something in her daughter's ear, silencing her.

Gray fought the urge to look at Charlie. Instead, he focused on the task at hand. "Do you know where the French ship was headed?"

"Not for certain, but it was a small coastal vessel and would not have been able to go far. It must have stopped in the nearest port."

"And where was that?"

"Marseille."

Damn and blast. He was going back to France.

* * *

ANTHONY GRAYLOCKE WAS AVOIDING HER AGAIN.

Throughout the trip down the coast, Charlie had savored the respite from him. When they were near, the only thing she could think about was their moment in the smugglers' cellar when she had almost kissed him, but he had pulled away. If he didn't enjoy her company, she didn't want his, either.

But she did want information, and that seemed to be the very last thing she could extract from him. He spent most of his waking hours above deck with the crew, where he'd warned her never to venture unescorted.

Yet every time she tried to approach him, he concocted some task that required his attention and excused himself from her presence. He didn't seem to care a whit if he left her alone with the crew, so long as he didn't have to endure her company.

No longer. She was getting answers from him even if she had to pry the words out of his mouth. Fortunately, the sea was calm, so she didn't slip and slide across the deck. The sun warmed the back of her neck. "Captain Graylocke," she called, shading her eyes as she searched for him. She tried to remain on his good side this morning, since her other tactics didn't appear to be working.

She heard a sigh that must have been his. She spotted him by the bow, up on the deck above. Gathering her skirts in one hand, she swiftly joined him. He was alone, for the moment.

"Charlie, please go back to your cabin. I have a crew to oversee. I don't have time to talk."

As she found her footing on the deck, she dropped her skirts and crossed her arms. "I have a right to know what is happening. Have you made contact with any other ships that might have seen Papa? Are we getting close to Marseille?"

He stepped closer. His body surrounded her, the heat soaking into her like the sun. She took a step back. The edge of her foot slipped on the ledge, and she nearly careened off onto the main deck. He caught her, pressing her against his body for a moment before he took a step back and released her, safely away from the edge. He didn't move away.

Her cheeks flushed, she averted her gaze. "Thank you."

"My pleasure," he said stiffly. "Now kindly return to your cabin."

She stiffened her spine. "No. Not until you tell me something. I'm going mad, locked away at all hours of the day. I need to feel as if I'm doing something."

"Your role at the moment is to wait."

Wait. She hated that word. "How long do I have to

wait?" It had been days since they'd last made port, and she felt of no use in the middle of the ocean.

A young man at the top of the mast shouted out a warning. Anthony crossed to the side of the deck and claimed a spyglass from his holster. He turned it toward the shore. Whatever he saw there brought a grimace to his face. He handed her the glass. "See for yourself."

As she raised it to her eye, she scanned the coastline and found a bustling port.

"I reckon you only have an hour or two of waiting left."

12

*A*s before, Anthony insisted upon sailing past the city and finding a sheltered cove before he set down the anchor. Why, Charlie couldn't fathom. They resided on a French ship. It wouldn't be any more noticeable in port than the dozen others that looked identical.

However, Anthony refused to be swayed, so when Charlie set foot on solid land again, it was once more on a sheltered beach. She brooded as she followed Anthony during the half-hour walk before Marseille came into view.

The city was magnificent. An enormous citadel surrounded by a stone wall perched on the edge of a horseshoe-like city surrounding the harbor. Although it was much smaller than London, Marseille was a sight to behold, nonetheless. As they approached, Anthony became more and more tense. His shoulders turned rigid ahead of her and Mama.

Charlie shortened the distance between them and touched his elbow. "What's bothering you? Do you expect trouble?"

He glanced from her to Mama and back. "Yes," he answered, his voice curt. "I might not be in uniform, but nothing can hide my military bearing. I'm no spy."

Mama stepped up to his other side. "No, but I am. I'll handle the questions inside town. All I ask is that you keep your eyes and ears open."

Anthony nodded. "Stay close," he commanded as he resumed walking.

Trotting to keep pace with his easy lope, Charlie said, "If the authorities will know you for a military man, shouldn't we be trying to keep our distance, in case the worst should happen?"

Anthony scowled. "And what if they notice you for an English lady?"

Charlie laughed. "I'm nobody. I wouldn't even garner a full dance card if my sister hadn't married your brother."

He glanced at her quickly then away and muttered something under his breath that sounded similar to "I very much doubt that."

"I beg your pardon?" Charlie asked. "I didn't quite catch that."

He offered her a terse command. "Stay close, and don't speak unless spoken to."

Charlie bristled but clamped her lips shut. If he didn't want her to speak, she wouldn't—at least, not to him.

Mama took the lead as they entered the city, and she began her search in the dockside taverns. At this hour, the fishermen were all at sea, finding their next catch. Most of those employed at other tasks were hard at work, keeping them away from the taverns. Save for a few travelers and the occasional local with a free afternoon, the eateries they visited were, for the most part, empty.

As afternoon bled into evening, that changed. More and more locals arrived, as well as those who'd slept the morning away. Businessmen conducting meals and interviews claimed the shadowed tables that afforded the most privacy. As hard as Charlie searched, she couldn't see Papa anywhere, but she wondered if she would recognize him. It had been years since they'd last spoken.

Mama left them at a table in the last tavern, which smelled strongly of fish, as she went to fetch drinks and make friends with the salty-looking men sitting along the bar counter. Charlie peered around for a mark of her own, hoping for a young man she could charm into giving details about the people he'd seen in the tavern recently. Choosing such a man was made even more difficult when Anthony loomed over her shoulder, glowering at anyone who dared to look them in the eye.

A rakish young man entered the tavern, scanning the interior with an appraising eye. He would do. With a smile and a flirtatious touch to the arm, Charlie would be able to coax him into sharing his every secret, if she could separate herself from Anthony long enough to keep him from glaring at the newcomer.

As she sidled around the table, trying to put some distance between them, a serving girl sashayed up to Anthony and asked him if he needed anything. From the purr of her voice, she wasn't asking him about food or drink. Charlie's stomach shrank and she abandoned her mark in order to glance sidelong at Anthony, wondering if he would take the invitation.

Charlie had no right to be jealous. He was a talented kisser, but he'd shown no interest in repeating their kiss, and she didn't want him to. He—and every other man—would only come between her and the adventure she so longed to experience. She was not going to give up that chance in order to play the demure wife and mother. Maybe someday, but not now.

Anthony could kiss whomever he wanted. Even better if doing so provided them with the information they sought. She turned away, her stomach churning, and pretended not to notice the flirtation unfolding mere feet away.

He answered the serving girl in stilted French. "Thank you, but my friend is getting all we need."

The woman frowned. The flirtatious way she leaned closer to him changed. She straightened and held her arm around her middle. "You have an intriguing accent."

No, he didn't. He had a British accent. *Blast!* Charlie swung her hips and tried to smile as she rounded the table. She laid her hand on Anthony's arm. Her heart thundered, but she battled the urge to spew the first words to come to her lips. She rehearsed them first, making sure she knew the proper vocabulary for what she wanted to say before she uttered the words out loud. The roaring in her ears didn't help her think, nor her mounting panic.

Imitate Mama. Smoothly, she said, "He hasn't been in France long. My sweet man is Bavarian." She thought that Bavaria was still on France's side in the coalition, but Charlie couldn't remember. Before she'd learned that Mama was a spy, she hadn't paid much attention to the war at all.

She wondered if she should have phrased that differently. Maybe she should have sought to distract the serving girl with an entirely different topic. The woman narrowed her eyes at Anthony and didn't seem convinced.

Fortunately, Mama arrived with three glasses of wine. She set them down on the table and smiled at the serving girl. "Thank you, but we have already been served."

As the young woman marched away, Mama's smile faded. She turned to Charlie and Anthony. "What happened? You weren't supposed to speak."

Charlie's stomach dropped, because that was precisely what she had meant to do, regardless. If Anthony hadn't bungled the answer to the serving girl, Charlie might have made a fool of herself with that rakish fop.

No. Her French was better than Anthony's. So long as she rehearsed what she meant to say in her head and carefully chose her words, she would have been fine. Granted, the man she combed for information might have thought her a bit slow of wit. All the better—Mama had taught her that once someone made a preliminary judgment of a person, they were more likely to overlook suspicious behavior and excuse it as part of their initial judgment.

Anthony grimaced as he answered Mama in a low murmur. "She asked me a question. Was I supposed to ignore her?"

Would the serving girl have approached to flirt with him if Charlie hadn't drifted away? She swallowed the question and asked, "Did you find anything?"

"Yes. I have an address. I wanted us to sit and have a drink so that we didn't arouse suspicion, but that might no longer be possible. Come."

Charlie fought to keep from grinning. With an address, they would find Papa, at long last.

GRAY CALLED HIMSELF SEVEN KINDS OF STUPID AS he followed Mrs. Vale up a narrow staircase to the rooms above the tavern—or inn, as it turned out. She counted the doors under her breath in French as she found the right one. The muscles in his shoulders knotted as he took up position behind her. Charlie stood to his right, dancing from foot to foot.

Mrs. Vale knocked.

A weak male voice called from within. "Who is there?"

"The innkeeper sent me," Mrs. Vale answered in the same language, French. "Will you please open the door, sir?"

A pause lengthened into a tension-filled silence. Gray glanced toward the stairs, from which they had ascended, wondering whether the serving maid had called for the French authorities, or if she had accepted Charlie's ludicrous tale that he was Bavarian. If the serving maid had ever spoken to a Bavarian, she would know that his accent wasn't remotely similar. He had crossed paths with one or two during his career in the Royal Navy.

The click of a lock returned his attention to the door and the man behind it. Gray tensed. This could be Mr. Vale, but he could have nearly exposed them in pursuit of a red herring, too. Slowly, the door opened a crack to reveal a sliver of a man. He had a receding hairline, brown hair, and bags around his eyes. It was those eyes, blue like Charlie's, that convinced Gray that they had found the right man.

The moment Mr. Vale beheld his wife, his eyes widened, and he opened the door. "Louisa?"

Next to Gray, Charlie bunched as if she meant to throw herself at the man, presumably her father. Gray laid a restraining hand on her arm and said sharply in English, "We don't have time for a happy reunion. I have a dinghy waiting in a cove outside Marseille and a ship to take us back to England. We must leave."

Both Mrs. Vale and her daughter seemed reluctant, but they complied with Gray's urgent tone. Mr. Vale took only a moment to kiss his wife and then grab a satchel containing his belongings before he exited into the hall. He cast his wife a sidelong look before he joined Gray in the corridor.

To Gray's surprise, Mr. Vale didn't question his presence. Either he recognized Gray's black hair, build, and features for a Graylocke, or he trusted that his wife and daughter would choose a trustworthy ally. "Where are we off to?" the older man asked in smooth French.

Either there was over a fifteen-year age gap between him and his wife, or Mr. Vale was so fatigued and under so much stress that he showed signs of age beyond his years. The slump of his shoulders despite his trim build, the bags around his eyes, and the lines around his mouth and nose all combined to make him look to be in his midsixties.

Gray didn't comment on the signs of fatigue in the man's bearing. Instead, he answered the question succinctly as he led toward the stairs. However, he'd barely informed the man of the cove where the French barque resided when, midway down the steps into the common room below, he caught sight of a French uniform. *Hell and damnation.* The serving maid hadn't believed Charlie's tale, after all.

Mr. Vale put a restraining hand on Gray's sleeve. "I know a back exit. Follow me."

Gray didn't argue. He hoped that Charlie's father was trustworthy, because at the moment he was putting his and the Vales' lives in the other man's hands. Charlie looked as pale as snow as he passed her.

"What happened?" she whispered to Gray in English.

He spoke only two words, but they were enough to render her silent. "French soldiers." When she pressed her lips together, her eyes wide and frightened, he considering trying those two words in the future, when they next had an argument. It might earn him a moment's respite to collect his thoughts.

He didn't have time to think now. Sliding his hand into his pocket, where his pistol resided, Anthony followed Mr. Vale along the corridor to a back staircase that exited into the open air. He and the Vales moved swiftly and silently. His heart beat so loudly, it was a wonder the French authorities didn't hear it and come barreling around the building.

On the street, he followed Mr. Vale's lead and offered his arm to Charlie. If they acted like two couples strolling along the street, they would be less likely to be noticed as fugitives. Charlie's arm trembled as she slid it onto his. He laid his hand atop hers and squeezed, attempting a reassuring smile. It felt weak.

As they reached the corner of the building he heard a shout in French. He couldn't decipher the rapid words, but when he glanced over his shoulder, he found the serving maid pointing an officer in his direction.

"Follow me," Mr. Vale shouted. He clasped his wife's hand and bolted down the street.

"What—" The word gushed from Charlie's mouth as Gray did the same with her.

"No questions. Run!"

When Charlie staggered over the hem of her dress, he nearly tossed her over his shoulder and carried her. A moment later, she wrestled her skirt into submission and draped the tail over her forearm. He released her hand and dropped his palm to the small of her back, steering her after her parents.

Although neither he nor the Vale women knew the layout of Marseille, Mr. Vale must have taken some time upon arrival to become familiar with the terrain.

He led them through alley after alley. They

jumped the fences and crossed private, fenced-in yards, taking turn after turn to throw off their pursuers. In fact, Gray was certain that at some point they were heading into the heart of Marseille, not away from it. When they reached the edge of the city, relief swept through him. It weakened his knees, but he pushed on. They weren't out of danger yet.

He took the lead. With Charlie at his heels, he followed the same path they'd taken into the city. Although he continually glanced over his shoulder, he saw no signs of pursuit from the French authorities.

He still didn't consider them safe. The moment they reached the cove, he ushered them into the dinghy. "Hurry. I want to be on the ship and weigh anchor before the French navy comes down upon us."

For once, Charlie didn't argue. She jumped into the boat and threw her arms around her father as he did the same. Gray shoved the boat into the water, hopped into it with the Vale family, and rowed for all he was worth.

They didn't have a moment to lose.

13

*L*ieutenant Stills stood in the shadow of the nearest mast, his hands clasped behind his back, as he watched Mama and Papa embrace tearfully. Charlie hugged herself as she waited for her turn. It had been years since she'd seen Papa. Years. She missed him. She blinked away tears.

Anthony crossed to stand next to her. He said nothing, so she remained silent. Around them, the crew hurried to turn the ship north and get underway. With the chaos of activity, it felt like Charlie stood in the eye of a storm.

Anthony brushed his hand over her shoulder, a warm reminder of his presence. "We did it."

She wondered if they really had. They still weren't safe in England, and the French navy might give chase.

Smiling, Mama and Papa parted. He turned to

Charlie and beckoned her closer. She raced into his embrace. "You've grown," he whispered as he hugged her.

"Perhaps you've shrunk," she teased. Her words emerged a bit watery. She brushed her tears away. This was a happy moment, and tears had no place here. But she'd missed Papa so much.

Anthony cleared his throat, standing closer than expected. "Perhaps you ought to adjourn to the captain's quarters."

"Yes, of course." Papa nodded.

As Mama showed him the way, Anthony stepped back to let Charlie follow. She hoisted her skirts so she wouldn't trip over them on the rolling deck and squeezed into the captain's quarters after her parents. Anthony, on her heels, shouted for Lieutenant Stills to remain on deck. "Let me know the moment you see a French flag!"

"Do you expect trouble, sir?"

"Be vigilant, just in case."

Charlie's stomach squeezed as if it were wringing out a wet rag. Her courage poured away from her. Seeing Marseille had been wonderful. She would have happily strolled along the streets for hours, admiring the vista and buildings. But the consequences of stepping foot in the city—the fear and threat of violence—

that wasn't adventure. That was war. She was ready to go home.

To her surprise, Anthony followed her into the captain's quarters with Mama and Papa. The room was small, and even with her parents sitting on the bed —or, in this case, Papa standing beside it before Mama laid a hand on his arm and begged him to sit next to her—there was precious little room for Charlie and Anthony. He shut the door behind him. They stood shoulder to shoulder. The heat of his body sank into hers, simultaneously bringing her comfort and an increased awareness of him.

Anthony said, "Forgive the intrusion. I'll leave you to your reunion in a moment, but if the information you have is of a sensitive nature to Britain, you must share it in case we are separated."

Papa sat straighter, throwing back his shoulders. "Of course." He looked between Charlie and Mama. "How much have you been told about Monsieur V?"

"He was the French spymaster in London," Charlie volunteered. "Lucy captured him a couple months ago—"

"Lucy did *what*?"

Charlie bit her lip to keep from laughing at the shocked and appalled look on Anthony's face. "Are you afraid your little sister is going to outstrip your daring deeds?"

"No." His voice was weak. He looked a bit pale.

She took pity on him and patted his arm. "You needn't worry. She and her husband have retired."

"Retired from what?"

"Spying, of course."

If anything, that made him look a bit gray. "She was a spy?"

"Briefly," Charlie answered without hesitation.

Mama elaborated, "She was never formally trained, but she took it upon herself to locate and arrange the capture of Monsieur V, with the help of her husband. He was a spy for much longer but retired after that mission. Even so, the duke was far from happy to hear of her involvement."

"I imagine so," Anthony said weakly.

Papa seemed confused at the turn in the conversation. Charlie smiled and returned to answering his question.

"Monsieur V was killed during the arrest, though."

"Not precisely," Mama hedged. "He died during transport to Lord Strickland for questioning."

"It amounts to the same thing," she insisted. "He is dead."

"Yes," Papa said, warming to this new topic. "However, before he died, I believe he alluded to the existence of a plot he'd set into play. I received instructions in France to look into such a plot and see if I could uncover it."

Charlie leaned forward. "And you did?"

Papa nodded. "A French spy, formerly posted in England, took refuge in Paris. With Monsieur V's death, the spy network in place in London is beginning to crumble."

Charlie grinned, assuming that was good news for Britain.

"I have a source in the French spy network in Paris, and I managed to learn the identity of this spy. It took a bit of work to cozy up to her, but I managed to convince her I was a friend and glean what she knew about Monsieur V. She left because she feared Lord Strickland knew of her true allegiance, and with no one to report to in London, it was no longer safe for her. Her part in Monsieur V's plan was done. She hired the assassin."

Charlie swallowed, wondering what the French plot to assassinate Lord Strickland meant for England. "When does this assassination take place?"

"Soon." Papa rubbed a hand across his face and looked at Mama. "I can't be more precise than that. She grew suspicious of me, and I had to leave Paris as soon as possible. They nearly caught me on the coast, so I took the first ship out and tried to go into hiding again, which is where you found me." He sighed. "I guess I wasn't careful enough."

"Or we were lucky," Anthony said, his voice soft. "I don't know if the Portuguese captain would have disclosed the same information to the French as he did to me."

Mama laid her hand on Papa's sleeve. Wrinkles formed around her eyes, and her mouth was thin. "What can you tell us about the assassination? Do you know the location?"

Papa deflated. His shoulders slumped, and he looked haggard. "I don't know where, precisely. Somewhere public, among friends, to prove their reach knows no bounds."

Charlie turned to Anthony. "Lord Strickland's life is in danger. We must reach London as soon as possible and warn him."

Papa frowned. "Strickland? He's not the one in danger."

"Don't be absurd. Of course he is. I have a missive —" Charlie reached for her bodice, only to recall that she'd delivered that paper to Anthony. She turned to him. "Do you have it with you?"

Whatever Anthony intended to answer, Papa cut

him off. "Lord Strickland is the figurehead, the person shown to the public. The true Commander of Spies works anonymously from the shadows, for their own safety. Somehow, Monsieur V learned this person's true identity, and the French mean to eliminate them at all costs."

Charlie bit her lip. "If Lord Strickland isn't the target, who is?"

Papa glanced briefly at Anthony before he answered, his expression hard. "Lady Evelyn Graylocke."

14

G ray strode the length of the ship that wasn't even his, earning the quizzical looks of his men. It brought him no solace. His ears still rang from the news Mr. Vale had delivered. It couldn't possibly be true. His mother couldn't be Britain's spymaster... could she?

Stills met him on the quarterdeck. "Is something amiss, sir? The man we brought aboard—"

"Mr. Vale," Gray supplied. "He is Mrs. Vale's husband and Miss Vale's father."

"Did he deliver some unsavory news? I know you seem to have a preference for Miss Vale, but if she's to be married to someone else..."

"I beg your pardon?" Gray shook his head. "I have no preference for Miss Vale. Quite the opposite. She is—"

"Captivating?" Stills grinned. "I find her rather comely, myself."

Gray scowled. "She is a guest on this ship. I won't tolerate any untoward behavior."

Stills smirked. "Of course not, sir. If she's not the source of your troubles, then what ails you?"

Rubbing his temple, Gray sighed, considering how much he should disclose. "We must return to England with all possible haste. Mr. Vale has information that suggests our Commander of Spies is in peril."

With a raised eyebrow, Stills remarked, "What of Miss Vale's wedding? Or will that not be going forward as planned, after all? Better news for you, sir." He winked.

Gray fought a grimace. "At the moment, our only concern is returning to England. You have your orders." His voice was sharp. He turned away before his second-in-command noticed the fear that permeated his every muscle.

His mother was in mortal danger. He'd already lost a father. He didn't know what to do, save for urging his crew to as great a speed as possible. Suddenly, he knew precisely the terror Charlie felt upon setting foot on his ship. No wonder she had been so insistent. If he hadn't known that his crew was performing their jobs with the utmost speed and accuracy, he would have been hounding the man in charge for information, too.

Parting ways with Stills on the quarterdeck, Gray retreated to where he would not be seen—his cabin below deck. It was squished and claustrophobic, but he doubted it would be any easier to breathe above deck when he had his mother's life dangling in front of him.

He had to believe that Morgan would keep her safe.

Morgan served as a spymaster of sorts within England, curating information from reports and training new spies. His wife, the duchess, invented gadgets to aid their endeavors. His younger brother, Gideon, had created a truth serum with his wife, and both continued to serve as field agents in London. Tristan's tenure as a field agent predated Morgan's. Gray was the only Graylocke who *hadn't* served as a spy in some capacity.

Perhaps that was why Mother had been so adamant that he refrain from joining the Royal Navy, because she'd hoped for him to carry on the family tradition of spying, instead.

Gray was no spy. Subterfuge wasn't his strong point—as evidenced by the fact that he'd told Lieutenant Stills more than perhaps he should have. No one had sworn him to secrecy, but this was sensitive information. The fewer people who knew, the less chance there would be of someone remarking out of turn.

In both his personal and professional lives, he preferred to handle himself in a straightforward manner. He liked dealings that laid out the honorable rules. Even war had rules, such as taking prisoners whenever possible rather than killing out of hand.

Though, given the way Morgan had chafed to serve his country when Gray had joined the Royal Navy, he wasn't surprised to find that his older brother had found another way to serve. What surprised him was Mother. His own *mother* was a spy, and no one had told him. Given Charlie's shock at the news, Mother hadn't told anyone. He wondered how long had she been doing this and whether it had predated his father's death.

As he descended to his cabin, he stopped short. From the moment she'd learned his name, Charlie had started babbling about his brothers. She'd known about their involvement in the spy network, even if she hadn't known about his mother. If he wanted answers, perhaps he ought to turn to her. He crossed to the neighboring door and knocked. "Charlie?"

"Come in." She sounded distracted.

Opening the door cautiously, he entered. He was

surprised to find her curled up beneath the porthole, struggling to catch the ambient outdoor light as she embroidered what looked to be a man's jacket. It appeared nearly complete, likely a product of his insisting she remain in her cabin at all hours. Although he was no expert, the needlework looked superb.

"Anthony." She swiftly tied off the thread and snapped the excess between her teeth. She laid the cloth on her lap and sat up straighter on the bed. "Come in. Are you all right? You seem unsettled."

Unsettled couldn't begin to describe the emotions he felt at that moment. He stepped into the room and shut the door. She was embroidering. Not only that, but she was good at it. For the first time since they'd met, he wondered if he knew her at all. Embroidery was such a ladylike pastime. And yet the brazen, outspoken, sometimes belligerent, *unladylike* woman voluntarily spent her time doing such delicate work.

Maybe he had he been wrong about her. She *could* be more suited to him than he'd thought at first. His mother was the most ladylike woman he knew... and yet it turned out that she was not only a spy, but she commanded the entire network. He didn't know what to think of her anymore, let alone what to think of Charlie, also involved in spying and with more ladylike qualities than he'd originally thought. And unlike with the mousy woman he'd always envisioned marrying, he could happily carry on a conversation with Charlie. Sometimes they argued, but she was never boring. She was wild like him, like the part of himself he had been trying to subdue for years. If she could be wild and ladylike all at once...

What was he thinking? His world had turned on end this afternoon. He didn't know what to think about anything. Not about himself, his future, or the woman whose chambers he had entered alone.

She scurried to one side of the bed to make room for him at its foot. "Come. Sit down before you fall down."

Do I look that out of sorts? He complied without argument.

When he did, she reached out and took his hand. Her fingers were bare, and her heat felt too good. He almost pulled her closer. "Is it your mother?"

He nodded. "And my brothers. And Lucy... everything. I hadn't the faintest idea that they were involved in this. They never told me."

"If it eases your mind, I think most have only joined up in the last year. That's when I learned about this—because of Freddie."

Holding her hand between both of his, he twisted to look at her. One of her curls had fallen free of her coiffure and clung to the corner of her mouth. She didn't appear to notice. He resisted the urge to brush it away. "Is your sister a spy as well?"

Charlie shook her head. "She was, briefly. Well, Lord Harker—our guardian—tricked her into spying for the French and trying to steal something from your brother. She and Tristan fell in love instead, and he sorted everything out. She helps him if she can, but she's confessed to me that she doesn't think she's suited for spy work. It's why she's never asked Morgan for training."

"Have you?"

"Asked to become a spy?" Charlie laughed. "No. Sneaking into people's bedrooms isn't my idea of adventure. For a long time, I thought Mama had retired as well, but she told me she's been doing smaller tasks, such as keeping an eye on Lucy."

Gray smirked. "Lucy does need to be watched."

"She isn't half as reckless as you Graylocke men seem to think, but before Monsieur V was killed, there was some need." Charlie's mouth twisted, but that stubborn curl clung to the corner. "No one told me, but in January she managed to see Monsieur V's face. No other spy had done that, so she was the only person able to identify him. Morgan wanted to keep her safe."

He heaved a sigh. "Spies… " He shook his head.

He still couldn't fathom it.

"They do good work."

"I never said otherwise." He admired the shape of her hand, nestled in his bigger palm. Her fingers looked so delicate, much the way she seemed at first glance. But she was stronger than she appeared, though he hadn't noticed that at first. She was brave, too. She'd risked her life to find her father. Now, she risked it to save his mother. She had a big heart.

She squeezed his hand and smiled. "Let it sink in. It's quite a shock, I know. Before Freddie married Tristan, I had no idea that a spy network existed in England, let alone that Mama was a part of it. Give it time, and you'll start to connect little things that you dismissed earlier."

His gaze fastened on her mouth once more and on that errant curl, teasing him. He'd dismissed her, from the moment they'd met. He shouldn't have. Unable to resist any longer, he lifted one hand to tuck that strand of hair behind her ear.

Her blue eyes darkened. "Thank you," she whispered.

He cupped her cheek, slowly leaning forward. He didn't trust himself to speak, to ask for the kiss he burned to take. Charlie answered his hesitancy by closing her eyes and turning her mouth up to meet his.

He kissed her. Sweet at first, but when he recalled their kiss mere feet away, desire gripped him. He deepened the kiss, surrendering to the sensation of her mouth. Charlie met him with every bit as much passion and eagerness as he felt. When she twined her arms around his neck and pulled him close, he bore her back toward the bed. She had him aflame. He ran his hand over her side, learning the shape and dip of her body.

When she threw her head back, gasping for air as she made a strangled noise, clarity returned in a bracing flood. Given another moment, he would have searched out the buttons on her dress. He thrust himself away.

"Anthony?" A furrow formed between her eyebrows, making her look uncertain.

"Forgive me. I never should have…"

Afraid of what he might do if he remained, he beat a hasty retreat. The moment the salty sea air on deck buffeted him, he berated himself for his weakness. Charlie was under his protection. It was his duty to keep her safe, not accost her. No matter what, he needed to keep his distance in order to ensure what had nearly happened between them never happened again, even if she was more ladylike than he'd thought and more alluring than he cared to admit.

15

The ship wasn't sailing fast enough for Gray's tastes, not with his mother's life in jeopardy. For days, he'd haunted the deck, willing the wind to fill the sails and push them north faster. What if they were too late?

"Anthony?"

He turned at Charlie's voice. She stood at the edge of the deck, near to the captain's quarters. No doubt she'd just exited from another day spent reacquainting herself with her father. He clasped his hands behind him tightly, burying the surge of jealousy that rippled through him. Not at another man monopolizing her time—at the fact that, after thinking her father dead, she had the opportunity to reunite with him. It was a precious thing.

Gray wondered whether his own father would be

proud of him, now that he'd become the upright, dutiful captain. Gray had always thought so, but... Mother appeared demure and ladylike until he learned of her involvement in the spy network. No, *running* the spy network. Father could have hidden a wild side of himself, too. Perhaps Gray was more like his father than he knew. Steeling himself, he crossed to Charlie. He stopped out of arm's reach, wondering what he should he say to her.

When she nibbled on her lower lip, the memory of their kiss haunted him. "Have you been avoiding me?"

Yes. "Of course not. I have work to do."

She opened her mouth to argue.

The ship lurched as a sound halfway between a rumble and a grating filled the air. Gray fought to catch his balance as the ship came to an abrupt stop. He barely found his feet in time to catch Charlie as she pitched forward into his arms.

The feel of her body was torture. Fortunately, he had an excuse to step away. He rounded on the helmsman. "What in the blazes is going on?"

The young man flushed a plum color. "Forgive me, Captain, but... I think we've run aground."

Gray swore vehemently and commanded his crew to check the ship for damage.

* * *

THE FRENCH BARQUE WAS STURDILY MADE. Despite the abrupt halt, no holes needed to be patched in the hull. Aside from a few chips in the paint, everything seemed in working order, except for the fact that they couldn't move.

"We'll have to wait for the tide to come in," Lieutenant Stills informed him.

Gray gnashed his teeth. The delay was unacceptable. His mother's *life* was in danger. "Is there nothing we can do?"

"Unless you'd like to stand neck-deep in water and dry to dig the ship out, no."

It was the closest Stills had ever come to giving him sass. Clenching his fists, Gray rounded on the helmsman. "How did this happen?"

The pallid young man tugged on his forelock. "Forgive me, sir. The map was a bit wet, you see. The ink smudged, and I thought the shallow waters didn't come this far out."

Gray grabbed the map in question from the helmsman's proffered hands. The map was horribly smudged, more so than it should have been from the bit of drizzle they'd had of late. The lines marking the coast smeared until they were a quarter of an inch thick. In a map this size, that small margin accounted for miles. Stifling a sigh, he thrust the map back into the young man's hands. "Place this somewhere safe. You are relieved of duty at the helm until further notice. Find his replacement, and check if we have any other maps of the area," Gray snapped to his second-in-command.

"Yes, Captain. I'm afraid it won't solve our predicament for the moment. Until the waters deepen again, we'll have to remain here."

"I know," Gray answered, his voice tight. He turned away and paced the quarterdeck as he thought over their options.

With Mother unaware of the assassination attempt, he couldn't suffer to sit still. If they arrived hours too late... *No.* It wouldn't happen, because he wouldn't allow it. One way or another, he was going to ensure his mother's safety. The admiral had given him orders to see Charlie's mission to completion; it wasn't complete until his mother was safe and the spy network alerted to the threat.

The chances were slim that another ship would happen upon them and offer its assistance. Gray would have to find another way to carry on, if not by sea, then by land. Grabbing the spyglass, he turned it toward the shore and tried to gauge the distance. Less than a mile.

If the barque hadn't had such a deep keel, they wouldn't be mired in this situation. A smaller ship would have been able to navigate the shallower waters of the embankment with ease. A dinghy would have no trouble at all.

Returning the spyglass to its holster, he loped toward his quarters and searched out the money he kept with him. The bulk of his wages went into a bank in London, but he kept some coin on him in case of emergency. This certainly qualified. It would be enough for a horse, though the quality of beast he would find in a small British village was not as high stepping as the horseflesh at Tattersall's.

Grabbing a small satchel, he transferred his money and what belongings he thought he'd need into it before returning above deck. The crew and the Vales awaited his return.

Charlie intercepted him. "What's happened?"

"In brief, we're stuck."

Her eyes widened. "For how long?"

"A few hours. Less than a day, to be certain, though this close to shore we'd have to anchor throughout the night regardless of the tide. We're only mired as long as the tide is out. A bit extra water will free the keel from the sand, and the ship will be able to get underway again."

She pressed her lips together as she processed that information. "That doesn't sound terribly dire."

"It isn't. But it's a delay we cannot afford. I'm going ashore."

She squared her shoulders. "Very well. I'll go with you." Her chin was mulish; her face was set.

He couldn't allow her to accompany him. He stepped past her toward the dinghy. "I'll move faster alone. As soon as the tide is high enough and there's enough light, Lieutenant Stills will escort you and your parents to the mouth of the Thames. The barque won't be able to sail up the river, but you can catch a river-boat to take you to London. I hope you'll arrive sooner than me."

Charlie hiked up her skirts and dashed in front of him. Since they had been run aground, the deck moved very little and didn't set her off balance. "And what if we don't? I signed on to this mission, and I will see it through to the end. I won't slow you down."

He stepped closer, lowering his voice as he tried to reason with her. The hairs raised on the back of his neck with the force of the stares of her parents and the crew. Whispers eddied behind them, but he ignored them. "I can ride faster on my own. If you accompany me, we'll have to take more rests. Forgive me, but I doubt you're accustomed to riding for such long stints."

She raised her eyebrows, her mouth pursing. "And you are? You're a navy captain!"

Although she had a point, he was loath to admit it. "This is my mother's life in danger. I'll push through."

"So will I—"

"Charlie." He caught and held her gaze, trying to beg her to see sense without using words.

It didn't work. Her eyes hardened, and she drew herself up. "I have a personal stake in the outcome too, Anthony. She may not be my mother, but this past year she has welcomed me into her home and family as if she was. Lady Graylocke has been like a second mother to me. At times, even a mentor or confidante. She is my family, too, and I will not sit by and"—she scrunched her nose—"work on needlepoint when there is something I might be able to do to save her."

Her vehement tone rose as she spoke. By the last word, the air rang with her words. She rendered Gray speechless. He had never met a woman with such courage and determination. If Mother meant so much to her, he couldn't deny her.

Swallowing hard, he nodded. "Very well. We'll go together."

* * *

CHARLIE RELEASED THE BREATH SHE HELD. HE was giving in so easily, which wasn't like the stubborn navy captain she knew. After all, he seemed to delight in butting heads with her. She'd expected to have to do battle with him before he relented.

He grumbled, "But you'd best be able to keep up."

There was the stubborn, disgruntled man she knew. She smiled, triumphant. "I will. I promise."

Mama stepped up, clasping her hands in front of her in a white-knuckled grip. Papa followed, wearing the tailcoat Charlie had finished embroidering. He looked dashing, even if his breeches weren't of as fine a make.

Mama said, "Very well. I'll fetch our valises. Richard?"

"Of course, dear." Papa started for the captain's quarters.

"Wait." Anthony rubbed his forehead. "That won't work."

Charlie drew herself up. "Why not?"

"It's too many people," he told her. "The dinghy can only seat four, and one of those four needs to row it back to the ship for use in case of emergency."

"Then use another one," she insisted.

"We can't. This is a captured vessel, as you may recall. The others appear to have been damaged during the capture. They will be fixed at port, of course, but we haven't the time or materials to fix them now."

Charlie gritted her teeth. "I will not be left behind, Anthony."

He looked past her toward her parents. "Somebody must. It will not be me."

Papa and Mama exchanged a mournful look. They had only recently been reunited after years of separation. Charlie didn't know the horrors to which Papa had been subjected during his time as a British spy on French soil. However, she knew that Mama's role as spy in Lord Harker's household hadn't been an easy one. She'd watched her mother fade away, little by little, while her sister Freddie struggled to pick up the pieces.

Anthony added, "Someone will have to remain aboard, in any case. If you reach London before me, someone must be able to deliver the message themselves."

Lieutenant Stills didn't help the matter when he stepped forward. "I'm going with you as well, Captain. You may need my arm."

Biting her lip to contain the way her stomach dropped, Charlie fought not to say a word. How dare he claim a spot in the boat when there was precious little space to begin with. There was nothing Lieutenant Stills could offer that Papa or Mama couldn't.

Anthony's expression was hard as he answered, "Absolutely not. You are captain of this vessel upon my departure. It is your duty to remain with it."

The usually smiling man clasped his hands behind his back, utterly serious. "With all due respect, sir, I have been your second-in-command far longer than I have been captain of this vessel. It is my duty to see that you complete your assignment safely and offer my assistance. I will not be swayed."

When Mama shifted to brush an errant strand of hair out of her face, she caught Charlie's attention. Mama offered an encouraging smile. "Captain Graylocke will do everything he can to impart the message. We'll do our part."

"No." Charlie recoiled, wrapping her arms around herself. "I'm going with him!"

"Absolutely not," Mama said, her face set. "I am not going to let you go off alone."

"I won't be alone. Anthony will be with me. Do you honestly think he would let any harm befall me?"

Mama's expression hardened. She drew herself up, even though she only reached to Papa's shoulder. "He *is* the harm, my dear. Or don't you have a care for your reputation?"

"My reputation?" The crew, formerly whispering, grew oddly silent throughout the exchange. Charlie rubbed her arms to throw off the unease of so much scrutiny. "A woman's life is in danger, Mama. I don't much care for my reputation at the moment, no."

Laying a hand on Mama's shoulder, Papa said quietly, "Louisa, why don't you go with her? We'll be reunited again in London."

Charlie's heart pinched. Their reunion had been so brief. It was impossible, in any case. "There isn't enough room," she said. "Not since Lieutenant Stills has opted to join."

Anthony turned an arch expression on his second-in-command. The man's mien remained unflappable. He hadn't changed his mind, even knowing that he stood between them and a clear solution.

Mama stepped between Charlie and Lieutenant Stills. To the navy officer, she pleaded, "Sir, won't you reconsider? I would not ask if not for the safety of my daughter. Captain Graylocke has stated it; who will command the ship while you are away?"

Lieutenant Stills inclined his head. "I will leave the ship in the very capable hands of *my* second-in-command. I promise, your needs will be well met. However, I cannot reconsider my position. At best, I can give you my word that Miss Vale will come to no harm while under my and Captain Graylocke's protection."

Shaking her head, Mama crossed her arms and rounded on Charlie. "Then you absolutely cannot go. Alone with two men? It is unseemly!"

"You would go," Charlie protested. "How would that be any different? Simply because you are married?"

"Because I am older and wiser," Mama answered, her jaw clenched. Her eyes snapped with determination.

Unfortunately for her, she had raised a daughter every bit as stubborn. Charlie held her ground. "I don't care if it is unwise. I don't care if it will damage my reputation. All I care about is doing the right thing, and you can't stop me."

"You are still my daughter—"

"I'm old enough to make my own decisions!"

Harried, Mama turned to Papa. "Why aren't you saying anything? Help me talk some sense into her. Or do you want her to run off without us?"

"Of course I don't," Papa answered. He stepped forward to lay an arm around Mama's shoulders. "But Louisa, she's right. She isn't a child anymore. It's been very clear to me since we reunited that she is an accomplished, levelheaded young woman. She knows the dangers of this."

When he looked at Charlie as if in confirmation, she nodded. "I understand." Perhaps not the specifics, since she'd never gone tearing across the country in search of an assassin before, but she understood that there would be a certain level of danger. If not from Anthony—she trusted him wholeheartedly—then from brigands or highwaymen on the roads, savage animals in the forests, or even hazards from the weather. Charlie was willing to take that risk.

"Richard… " Mama didn't seem as willing to allow her to do so.

Papa raised his hand, stalling her. "This is precisely what happened between you and your mother shortly before we eloped. I know it's been one of your greatest regrets. Charlie has made up her mind, and it seems as though she means to go no matter what you try to say to dissuade her, so you might as well give her your blessing, lest it drive a wedge between the two of you."

Charlie straightened her spine. Papa was right. She wouldn't let Mama or anyone else stop her from doing this. She wasn't a child.

Mama's expression crumpled. Tears filled her eyes. Worry pinched Charlie's stomach. Quietly, Mama conceded, "If you're that set on going, I won't stop you."

The words seemed all but swallowed by the silence that followed. Mama wiped her eyes and looked up, meeting Charlie's gaze.

"Thank you." Charlie's words were every bit as soft. She didn't know what else to say.

Mama stepped forward to clasp her hands. "I'm worried about you, love." Tears leaked from the corners of her eyes.

Charlie couldn't remember the last time she had seen Mama cry. She was always so strong, so composed. Tears threatened to choke Charlie, too, but she blinked them away. She swallowed around the lump in her throat. "I know, Mama. I have to do this."

When she opened her arms, Charlie embraced her. Mama squeezed her tight as she confessed, "I don't want you to go alone, but I don't want to part in anger, either. I had an argument with my mother that caused a rift between us that lasted until the day she died. I still did what she forbade me to do." Pulling away, Mama cupped her daughter's cheeks. "I don't want that to happen with us, love. Please stay safe."

"I will." Charlie's voice was hoarse. She could barely speak around the constriction in her throat. "I won't be alone. Anthony will be with me. You trust him, don't you? I do."

Tears shining in her eyes, Mama turned to Anthony. "You'd better live up to your family name. If anything happens to her..."

He straightened, clasping his hands behind his back as he assumed a rigid posture. "You have my word. I will keep her safe."

Mama drew her arm around Charlie's shoulders and steered her toward her cabin. "Then, my dear, let's see you packed. I'll make sure you have everything you need."

"Quickly," Anthony reminded them in a curt tone. "It's nearly dark. We must set out as soon as possible."

Charlie's blood sang as reality set in. She was going on an adventure.

16

*T*hank the Lord that when Gray had promised to keep Charlie safe, he hadn't given his word that she would be comfortable. Ever since they'd left the dinghy behind and continued on foot to the coastal village where they purchased horses, their journey had been a rocky one.

The dwindling light had made for treacherous footing. More than once, Charlie had tripped over her skirts or a crevice in the path. Once, the injury had cost them minutes as he'd examined her ankle to her vociferous protests. It hadn't been broken nor, so far as he could tell, sprained, but even though she had waved off his assistance, her uneven gait from there on had warned him that the appendage continued to give her pain.

In the village, they'd stopped for a quick meal, and

after paying over three quarters of the blunt he and Stills had brought with them, they'd managed to part the villagers from three mangy nags. If he hadn't been so desperate for horses, he would never have bought the skinny, shaggy beasts that he feared at first wouldn't hold up to his weight.

However, although they were clearly malnourished, the placid beasts obeyed readily and bore his weight with aplomb. Without taxing Charlie's ankle any longer, they continued on their way. However, night upswept them before too long, rendering them all but blind. He carried a lantern on a long pole to light their path, but somehow they still had to stop for large stretches of time to search out the path where it became overgrown. And then, to crown their misery, it began to rain.

"We should have taken the road to London," Stills grumbled as he led the horses one by one to a thin ribbon of water for them to drink.

Gray pretended not to hear. He had chosen this path because it led to Tenwick Abbey, closer to the coastal town than London even if the roads were not as well-traveled. With luck, he would find his mother in residence there and he would be able to impart his warning with a clear conscience.

For the moment, he had the health of another stubborn woman to contend with. He positioned himself so his shoulders blocked the view of his second-in-command as he folded Charlie's damp skirt above her ankle. The appendage was clad in silk stockings, not quite sheer enough to judge the pallor of her skin beneath. "Has it been giving you grief?" he asked.

She pressed her lips together and shook her head. "I'll persevere."

He kept his eyes on her face as he gently poked at her ankle, searching for any spots that seemed unduly tender. He found one, but it produced only the barest cringe. She didn't flinch or yank her leg from his grasp.

When he finished and tucked her ankle beneath her skirt once more, she raised her eyebrows. "See? I'm no more than bruised, if that."

He crouched on his heels. The overhang of the tree over the thick, pronounced root where she sat shielded him somewhat from the steady rainfall. Given the gurgle in the distance, he suspected the storm would soon become much worse. He needed to find them shelter for the night before the weather worsened. An inn, if he could manage. Although farms dotted the countryside, he didn't think that Charlie would much appreciate bedding down in a hay loft. "You haven't been as talkative as usual."

She rubbed her face with both hands. He

suspected she did so to cover a yawn. He bit back one of his own. It had been a long day, and they had been traveling by land for hours.

"It's raining. What inclination I have to chatter has been washed away."

He grinned. "Is that the secret to rendering you speechless? I'll have to remember that for the next time we get in an argument."

She gave him an arch look, the corners of her mouth curling in a smirk. "It won't help you win."

From feet away, Stills called that he'd found the path once more. Gray stood, offering his hand to Charlie to help her to her feet. She accepted with grace. When she stood, she didn't appear to be favoring her ankle. He wondered how much of that composed mien was born of sheer stubbornness.

Renewing his conviction to seek out an inn with all possible haste, he helped her to her horse and lifted her into the sidesaddle. "Thank you," she said as she gathered her reins.

He mounted and followed Stills, who had taken command of the lantern. Gray didn't protest; his arm ached from holding it aloft, and he relished the respite. "How much longer can you ride?" he asked Charlie as they set off.

She straightened her spine. "As long as it takes."

Liar. She wasn't nearly the horsewoman he'd hoped. If her mount hadn't been so demure, she would have landed on her rump more than once. A rump that, given her unfamiliarity with riding, must be aching by now. Even his had started to give a twinge.

Although the obstinate woman seemed set on enduring whatever hardship befell them, he knew for everyone's sanity that he'd best find them a place to rest for the night—and soon.

* * *

A THIN BIRCH FREE FALLEN ACROSS THE PATH shouldn't have been cause for alarm. Bitters—the name Charlie had given to her horse because the color of his mane reminded her of the last dredges in the bottom of a teacup—was tall enough to step over the log with ease. However, the moment he hopped over and stumbled, her heart jumped into her throat.

She shrieked, echoing the horse's whinny. He danced sideways, in clear pain. Charlie dropped the reins and clutched twin handfuls of his mane to keep her seat. She nearly did, but as the horse stepped wrong again, he bucked.

"Charlie!"

She could barely see the mane in front of her, let

alone the man shouting her name. Her vision swam as panic gripped her. She struggled to hang on as the horse bucked again beneath her. She forgot to breathe.

A man's strong arms plucked her from her horse and deposited her in front of him. The hard wedge of the saddle dug painfully into her rump, but she didn't care. This mount didn't roll beneath her like a ship during a storm. She wrapped her arms around Anthony's warm torso and buried her face in his wet collar. He was no drier than she, but the heat of his body soaked into her and slowly relaxed her. Her shivers abated. Her heartbeat slowed to normal as he rubbed his palm over her back.

"Are you hurt?"

She shook her head, still buried in his collar.

Lieutenant Stills called, "Bad news, Captain. The horse seems to have thrown a shoe. We'll have to keep to a slow pace, and it won't be able to bear a rider."

Anthony swore under his breath. His arm tightened around her until he abruptly released her. She continued to cling to him.

"We can't ride like this," he said softly. "It isn't comfortable or practical. You'll have to sit behind me."

When she raised her gaze to him, she found his eyes dark in the pool of light cast by the lantern.

"You'll let me ride with you?" In her opinion, that was the very definition of not being able to keep up.

"You'll have to," he said matter-of-factly. "Your horse cannot bear your weight. He can scarcely bear his own."

She bit her lip and looked down. "Forgive me. I didn't mean to harm the horse."

The touch of his hand was cold as he dipped his index finger beneath her chin and used it to raise her gaze. For a moment, his touch lingered. His gaze fastened on her mouth. Did he fancy kissing her at that moment? She licked her lips, anticipating his touch.

Instead, he dropped his hand and cleared his throat. "I doubt it was anything you did. The shoe must not have been nailed on straight. These nags aren't in the best condition, so I wouldn't put it past that village to have done shoddy farrier work as well. Are you fit to move? I need to transfer you behind me if we're to continue."

Burying her disappointment over returning to the reality of their search, Charlie nodded. With Anthony's help, she moved to sit sidesaddle behind him. She wrapped her arms around his waist for balance as they set off again. His warmth and the lack of a need to concentrate on what she was doing made her sleepy.

When she cracked a yawn, Anthony said over his

shoulder, "Don't worry. I'll find us a place to weather out the night as soon as may be."

She almost resented the promise of a bed. When it came, she would have no more excuse to touch him.

* * *

GRAY HAD BEGUN TO DESPAIR OF FINDING anywhere to bed down, even the barn of a local farm. Fortunately, as the track widened and began to grow passable again, they came to a crossroads. At the crux was a shabby little inn, two stories tall. It would have to do.

The innkeeper didn't seem particularly pleased to be roused from bed after midnight. The proprietress's frown deepened as she noticed who was at her door. Her dress, hastily donned, gaped over her upper chest. Her hair resembled a bird's nest.

Gray straightened his shoulders. "Madam, I beg your pardon for arriving so late in the evening, but we are looking for a place to spend the night and rest our horses. I am Captain Graylocke of the Royal Navy, and this is Lieutenant Stills."

"And would she be your wife?" The woman's voice dripped with censure.

Charlie bristled. She drew herself up, no doubt to

deny the accusations, but Gray slung his arm around her shoulders and tucked her into his side. "She is," he lied. "You may address her as Mrs. Graylocke."

Given the way Charlie stiffened next to him, he would come to regret giving her that moniker, albeit temporarily. He only prayed that she wouldn't speak the truth. The innkeeper didn't seem likely to grant them shelter at this hour if she believed Charlie to be a fallen woman.

Fortunately, Charlie held her tongue—likely a testament to how exhausted she was. She leaned into Gray's embrace. He wondered if her ankle was giving her grief.

The innkeeper's face softened as she returned her attention to Charlie. "You poor dear, you're soaked to the skin. Why don't you come in and sit for a moment? I'll rouse my husband to tend your horses while I start a fire in two of our rooms. We'll see you and your husband settled straight away, Mrs. Graylocke, don't you fear."

Two rooms. Gray swore inwardly. He hadn't thought far enough ahead. In the *ton*, most husbands and wives kept separate rooms. However, they were far from London; she hadn't recognized him as a duke's son, or she would have jumped to accommodate him regardless of Charlie's fictitious position as his wife.

Now, if he wanted to keep up the ruse, he would have to share a bedroom with her.

To sleep in the same bed with her warm body next to him would be far too much temptation.

Heedless to the torture to which she subjected him, the innkeeper bustled into a modest common room filled with wooden tables and benches. Stills remained outside, holding the horses and the lantern while he found the stables. The only light inside the establishment came from a tallow candle perched atop the nearest table.

"How long have you two been married?" the older woman asked as she found a second candle and lit it from the wick of the first.

When Charlie looked a bit panicked, Gray answered for them both. "Not long," he said, biting off his words.

"On your honeymoon, are you?" For all her earlier sourness, she seemed in a remarkably amiable mood now. "I had wondered why a captain in the Royal Navy would be so far inland. I thought you gents never strayed from a port city like Brighton."

Gray smiled tightly. "It's true, I would never abandon my duty for anything less than life-changing."

When the innkeeper opened her mouth—perhaps to quiz them further—he cut her off.

"Forgive me, madam, but it is extraordinarily late, and we've been riding all afternoon in search of a proper inn. Could we beg you for the bed now?" He caught Charlie's hand, finding it cold. "And perhaps a cup of tea or something hot to eat if you have it."

"Oh, dear me, yes, of course. Let me go stoke those fires up first thing and wake my husband. Don't want your companion..."

"Lieutenant Stills," he supplied when she trailed off.

"Yes, don't want this Lieutenant Stills to be out in the rain any longer than necessary. I won't be long, I promise."

As she left, taking the second candle with her, Gray lowered himself onto a bench next to Charlie. He still held her hand. He warmed it between his, despite the fact that he was likely no warmer. What he wouldn't give for a hot bath. That, unfortunately, was impossible.

After a moment, Charlie whispered, "Thank you." When he looked at her askance, she elaborated. "I know you want to press on."

He switched to warming her other hand. "If we don't stop, we'll fall dead on our feet tomorrow. The horses, as well."

She didn't say anything further. When he was

done warming her hands, she retracted them onto her lap. He felt strangely bereft without them.

Stills entered shortly thereafter, soaked to the skin and looking as though he was near to dropping. Gray accepted his and Charlie's packs. Stills barely said two words before the proprietress returned to lead them to their rooms. "I'll cook you up a hot hash and bring it up straight away."

She showed Gray and Charlie to their room first—a blessing, for it meant that he would soon be rid of his wet clothes. Once he entered the small room, equipped only with a bed, a chair and writing desk, a bedside table, and a dressing screen in the corner, he recalled that he was sharing this room. Without looking at Charlie, he shut the door and offered her one of the satchels he carried.

"You should remove your wet clothes before you catch a chill."

She nodded and accepted the pack, peeking inside. The firelight from the hearth gave off a warm glow that lit across her cheekbones. Even with her hair limp and bedraggled, she looked beautiful. She toed off her slippers, keeping them by the door, before she tiptoed to the bed and set the satchel on the floor next to it. She extracted a long white nightgown. Despite the light pouring from the fire, she carried the candle from downstairs to the dressing screen. When she began to disrobe, the shadow of her figure showed through the screen.

Lud! He turned his back and bent to remove his boots, setting them next to her slippers. Despite his attempts to keep his thoughts on the fire, their mission, or what he intended to wear to bed—certainly more than his smallclothes, given that they now shared a room—he couldn't banish the image of her removing her dress.

When she stepped from behind the screen, the reality was no better. Her wet hair rendered the white fabric sheer in places near her shoulders and upper chest. The firelight seemed to make her eyes bluer and her cheeks rosier. Hastily, he plucked his clothes and retreated behind the screen. There was a small basin there with a bar of soap and a damp cloth. He used it to wash himself quickly before he donned new clothes and stepped out from behind the screen. When he did, he found Charlie seated at the writing desk, brushing her hair. The only place for him to sit was the narrow bed. He perched on the edge.

After a tense moment, he asked, "How is your ankle?" He tried valiantly not to look at her bare foot as he did.

She wagged the brush at him. "I'm in perfect

health, Anthony. I've already said as much multiple times."

He hadn't noticed a limp while she walked, but that didn't mean he wasn't concerned. She must be as saddle-sore as he was, but he couldn't possibly ask after the state of her bottom. The ankle would have to do.

His gaze plummeted to the hem of her night-gown. Her bare feet poked out the bottom. As he watched, she curled her toes in and tried to tuck them beneath the nightgown. A swatch of her ankle came into view as she rearranged the gown, including a faint purplish bruise. She had been hurt during the walk but appeared much too stubborn to admit it.

As he opened his mouth to push the topic further, a knock at the door interrupted them. Although he was clad in no more than his shirtsleeves and breeches, he crossed to the door and opened it. He tried to bar the view of Charlie.

The proprietress was there with two plates of the hash she'd promised, along with a steaming pot of tea. He accepted the tray and thanked her, promising to put the dishes outside the room when he'd finished.

When he turned, Charlie stepped away from the writing desk to give him room to set down the tray. She slipped past him toward her satchel to put away her hairbrush. "That smells divine. I know we ate in the last town, but I'm famished."

He smiled and poured her a cup of tea. When she settled on the edge of the bed, he passed it and the plate to her. "Traveling so much tends to work up an appetite."

He contemplated sitting next to her. He wouldn't be as tempted to ogle her neckline, but they would be far too close. He took the seat in front of the writing desk instead. He started to eat the hash, cubed chunks of meat cooked alongside cubed root vegetables, but he scarcely took two bites.

Now that they had stopped for the night, the day—and the week—caught up with him. His mother's life was in danger, and here he sat, idle with a hot plate of hash. If he'd been alone, he wouldn't have stopped. Perhaps he would have tried to trade in his horse for a fresh one and catch an hour's nap, but then he would be back in the saddle, pressing on to Tenwick Abbey and praying to find his mother there safe and sound. Instead, he had to think of Charlie's health. Even if she hadn't complained, he couldn't push them to exhaustion the way he might do himself.

He rubbed his forehead as he stared at his food, no longer hungry. What if he didn't make it in time?

Charlie's delicate touch to his knee returned him

to the present. Her eyes glimmered with concern when he raised his gaze. "We'll do everything we can. We will save her. Neither you nor I will settle for anything less."

Her voice held such a note of conviction that he suspected if he asked her to push on after an hour's rest she would willingly do so. He clasped her hand, taking what comfort she offered. Mother had touched her, as well. Perhaps she didn't love his mother in precisely the same way she loved her own, but she loved Mother all the same. He hadn't known how much he'd needed an ally in his worry before now. If he'd been alone... it wouldn't have been the same.

"Thank you." His voice was hoarse. He offered no other words. He had none to offer.

It was enough. Even after they returned to their meals and she retracted her hand, her presence in the room reminded him that he was not alone in this.

Despite his lack of appetite, he ate every scrap on his plate, wanting to keep his strength up. Charlie didn't quite finish hers, for all her pronouncement of hunger, but he didn't push her. Instead, he collected their plates and cups and set them outside the door, as instructed. Down the short corridor, another tray rested outside another room, presumably Stills's. Gray shut and locked the door.

When he turned, he found Charlie standing as well, wringing her hands, and she nibbled on her lower lip. Her hair had started to dry, fluffing out from her head and lightening in color. When she stopped nibbling on her lip, the rosy hue of her mouth beckoned to him. He swallowed hard as he relived their last kiss, and the one before. His reasons not to kiss her again were growing thinner by the day. "Which side would you like?"

Lawks! She thought he meant to sleep in bed next to her? A bed that size meant that he would be pressed intimately against her. The thought fired his blood. He crossed the room, and until he reached her, he didn't know what decision he would make. Kissing her could lead to... irrevocable things. He wanted her, unable to deny that fact any longer. But he still had his honor, his word.

He reached past her to take one of the two pillows. "I'll sleep on the floor."

Her blond eyelashes fluttered in front of her eyes as she blinked a few times in a row. "You aren't going to sleep in the bed?" She licked her lips, enticing him further.

He bit back a groan. She stood close enough for him to feel the heat of her body. Swallowing hard, he thrust the pillow between them as a shield against the temptation. "It wouldn't be proper."

She frowned. "Proper? Anthony, I trust you."

Therein lay the problem. She'd already shown him once that if he wanted to kiss her, she wouldn't stop him. Where was the line? Better he not risk crossing it.

"Perhaps you shouldn't." He leaned forward to kiss her soft cheek. "Good night, Charlie."

Tucking the pillow under his arm, he marched to the fire and stretched out in front of it. A moment later, the floorboards creaked, and Charlie draped the bed's thin coverlet over his body. When he twisted to thank her, his mouth dried at how near she was. She curled her toes.

"The bed has a sheet as well. I don't need it. Good night, Anthony."

As she climbed into bed, he faced the fire once more and tried to will himself asleep.

17

*W*ith summer in full bloom, Charlie shouldn't have woken cold. But the drizzle splattering against the wall of the inn seemed to have seeped into her very bones. Now that the fire had gone out, the room seemed still and gray. The threadbare sheet wasn't quite enough to keep her from shivering.

A moment later, the coverlet, still warm from Anthony's body heat, landed across her legs. Anthony straightened next, his posture rigid. He looked away, his expression hard as he stretched. "If you were cold, you should have kept the blanket."

Charlie gathered it to her chest, soaking up his residual body heat. "Perhaps you should have slept next to me and we both would have been warm."

He exhaled sharply as he looked at her, then away

again. Charlie held her breath. The invitation rippled in the air between them, much as it had last night.

Last night, she'd been all but certain that he would kiss her. She'd nearly asked him to. When she'd confessed to trusting him, she'd hoped that would be all the invitation he needed. Unfortunately, he'd chosen to be proper.

Her body hummed at the notion of sleeping alongside him, in his arms. When they'd arrived, he'd lied to the innkeeper and claimed that Charlie was his wife. A man slept next to his wife. He took other liberties while in bed, too. Liberties which, given Anthony's reluctance to sleep next to her, he was clearly afraid he might take.

Charlie wasn't afraid. One benefit to having a friend like Lucy, who was detailed in expressing her experiences, was that she always got a lengthy answer to her inquiries—including what it had felt like for Lucy to give herself, body and soul, to her husband.

Charlie might be virginal in body, not wanting to lose her freedom to any man, but she knew what awaited her that inevitable day she decided she'd had enough adventure.

The way her blood sang when Anthony stepped near felt eerily similar to the way she'd felt upon embarking on this adventure to find her father. Kissing

Anthony felt as much a victory as bringing Papa aboard the ship. Somehow, Charlie knew that the day Anthony decided to damn what was proper, he could take her to places she'd never been before.

However, the closest she'd been able to come to uttering an invitation of that magnitude had been to suggest that she trusted him. Trust that he did not place in himself. *Because you're an animal?* She'd almost parroted his words back at him, but she hadn't wanted to frighten him away. Unfortunately, she'd seemed to do that simply by existing.

And he seemed in a surly mood this morning because of it. Perhaps he was simply being a pigheaded dolt, due to lack of sleep from lying on the cold, hard floor. Or perhaps her snoring had kept him awake. The bed was so uncomfortable that she'd even snored loud enough to wake herself once. As she felt her cheeks heat, she snuggled deeper under the blankets.

He stared at her a moment more before opting to ignore the fact that she'd offered for him to sleep next to her in the next inn. "If you don't mind, I'll wash up first, then see about getting us some breakfast."

Charlie twisted to look out the window and gauge the time. Not long past dawn at her guess. If they'd slept more than four hours, she would be surprised.

Nevertheless, she nodded. "I don't mind." She

huddled beneath the blanket as he retreated behind the screen. As the warmth seeped into her, she struggled not to fall asleep. At home, she usually lay abed until noon. Her jaw cracked as she yawned, daydreaming of her soft bed in London or the one at Tenwick Abbey. When at home, she always slept through the night. What a blessing that would be, with Anthony mere feet away.

He took mere minutes to complete his washing and dressing. As he buttoned his jacket and tossed the oiled cloak around his shoulders, he crossed to the door. "I'll be in the common room below when you're finished. Please don't tarry."

He didn't look at her before he shut the door.

Had she imagined the longing and desire in his eyes last night? They'd only shared two kisses, and both times, he had been the one to end them. Now he refused to look in her direction. Perhaps she'd made a fool of herself by inviting him to share her bed.

"Forget him," she mumbled under her breath as she rose.

Unfortunately, that was much easier said than done, especially when she had to share a horse with him. When she emerged downstairs ten minutes later, she found Anthony pacing in front of two bowls of porridge.

Despite her lack of appetite, she tried to eat as quickly as he did while Lieutenant Stills informed them both of the fact that he had procured directions toward Tenwick Abbey from the inn, and the state of Charlie's horse. Without a farrier near the inn and with no mounts to spare, Charlie had no choice but to sit with Anthony as she had the day before. Her horse would be left behind to save them time.

Anthony said little, not a word of it to her. Even after they finished and settled their account, and he lifted her atop the rump of his gelding, he scarcely looked at her, let alone spoke. As he set a punishing pace for both horse and rider, she had no breath left to speak, in any case.

THE HORSE DANCED BENEATH GRAY, RESTLESS, AS he consulted his compass. He glanced at the sky, then back at his device, then swore. The obscenity made Charlie, seated behind him with her arms around his waist, jump and clutch him tighter. Her body pressed tight along his back, as it had for most of the day. He couldn't purge her from his thoughts for a minute before she dominated them again.

He'd spent most of the night awake, listening to

her fitful snore as he agonized over the future. He had to keep his focus on saving his mother, yet Charlie was always nearby, a temptation and a dangerous distraction.

"What's wrong?" she whispered, her voice low and intimate.

It pinched him in the gut. He swallowed before he announced, "Our directions were poor."

Mere feet away, Stills straightened atop his mount. "I followed the innkeeper's instructions to the letter—"

Gray held up a hand to silence further excuses. "I'm not blaming you, Stills. I should have known when the innkeeper didn't recognize my family name that she likely wouldn't know where Tenwick Abbey was located."

Charlie pressed her cheek into his shoulder. "So... we're lost?"

Yes. He feigned bravado. "Of course not. We're delayed, that's all. By my estimate, we've veered too far north, but if we turn around and take the track running east-west, we should be able to find an oft-traveled road that leads in the right direction."

To him, the confidence in his tone rang comically false. However, Charlie must have believed him because after a moment's hesitation, she suggested, "Then why are we dallying? Let's not waste time."

Lieutenant Stills didn't seem as convinced, but Gray didn't leave him room to argue. Turning his horse around, he prepared to dig in his heels. "You heard the woman. Let's not tarry."

His mother's life hung in the balance, after all. This delay was only one in a long line, none of which they could afford. No matter the cost, they had to reach Tenwick Abbey in all possible haste, even if they had to do so with Charlie sitting near enough behind him to rouse his thoughts and his ardor. Even if they reached their destination as soon as tomorrow—which now seemed impossible—this was going to be a very long trip.

18

The small stables at the rear of the ramshackle inn might have been able to comfortably hold six horses, if two of the stalls hadn't been filled to the brim with hay. Fortunately, this inn had even fewer patrons arriving by horse than the last, judging by the sparseness of the stables.

Or perhaps Gray should call the inn a tavern. The moment he, Charlie, and Lieutenant Stills stepped into the two-story building, they found the common room filled to capacity with local farmers and their progeny. The second story housed the owner's personal quarters, they were informed, and there was only a single room to be let. Gray suspected that had he not been the son of a duke, he wouldn't have been offered that room.

Putting his arm around Charlie's shoulders, he

smiled tightly. "My wife and I will take that room, then."

The stodgy innkeeper inclined his head and hunched his shoulders, the closest it seemed he would come to a bow. "Of course, my lord."

Gray bit the inside of his cheek to keep from flinching. As the son of a duke, he had always been addressed as Lord Graylocke or Master Anthony, if one of his brothers was present. However, that had been an accident of his birth; his title as captain had been earned, and he much preferred it. Nevertheless, if it earned them shelter for the night, he would have to hold his tongue on the matter.

At least until the innkeeper added, "And what of your man, sir? I can offer him the common room if he'd like to stretch out in front of the hearth once the rabble has left."

Gray gritted his teeth. "As I've said, my companion is *Lieutenant* Stills of the Royal Navy—"

Stills raised his hand, stalling Gray's correction. "The common room will do," he said stiffly.

The slosh of some liquid onto a floor that must be sticky with the leavings of the patrons made Gray wince. If Stills wanted to sleep on that, it was his decision to make. At least Gray could trust the floor of his room to be relatively clean. It had better be, or this son of a duke would raise a complaint to the innkeeper. After a day's hard riding in the vain attempt to get back on track, he was irritable and ready for sleep. He only hoped it would come easier than it had the night before.

"Might we inquire about supper?" he asked, his voice curt. "A private room, if you have one available."

The innkeeper wrung his hands as he confessed that they didn't typically offer a back room to patrons. At Gray's glare, he offered the family's personal dining room, which Gray accepted.

Since Stills was destined to remain in the common room all night, Gray insisted he take the night's meal with him and Charlie. She didn't complain. When he asked if she'd like to go up to their room and freshen up before the meal, she raised her eyebrows at him as though he'd offered her one of the horse's stalls instead. Every other woman of his acquaintance would have wanted to wash up before dinner—in fact, he would have as well if he'd had his usual change of clothing on hand. However, Charlie was not like other women. For instance, other women would not have held onto him without complaint as he'd pushed them so hard today.

Malnourished as they were, the horses couldn't continue such a pace indefinitely. He'd had to walk next to his horse from time to time, leading it while

Charlie rode or joined him on the ground despite his protests. She matched his long-legged stride, giving him no ammunition to use to convince her to ride. Although they'd taken frequent breaks at streams to water and rest the horses, the ten or fifteen minutes idled there hadn't given them time for a proper meal.

Through all this punishment, Charlie hadn't uttered a word of complaint. In fact, once or twice she'd even insisted she had rested enough and spurred them onward. She was made of sterner stuff than her delicate countenance suggested.

Nevertheless, by the time they three found themselves ensconced in the dining room, Gray barely had enough energy left to eat, let alone to attend to the conversation between Charlie and Stills. Stills, having gotten solid sleep in a bed, was much more alert than Gray and served the three of them their meal. Gray ate it without tasting it.

When Charlie tapped him on the arm, Gray was only too happy to bid his second-in-command good-night and stagger above stairs, where their room awaited. It was just as cramped as last night's room—more so, in fact, given that this one didn't come equipped with a hearth. The air was stale. Gray opened the small window to let in some of the balmy summer air. It wasn't raining today, and a dense humidity seemed to have curled around them, one that couldn't be dispersed by the robust wind.

Charlie led him by the elbow toward the screen in the corner of the room. "You wash up first tonight. You look dead on your feet."

He rubbed his face. "I'll be fine."

"Yes. You will be. Once you've had a solid night's sleep. We did well, finding an inn not long after dark."

He couldn't argue with that.

After she bullied him behind the screen, she rummaged in his satchel and found some folded clothes. She offered them over the top of the screen, her eyes averted despite the fact that he hadn't yet begun to undress. "Will these do?"

"I imagine they'll do admirably, thank you."

He changed quickly, lamenting the fact that the necessity to travel light meant that he had only one more set of clean clothes. He put them on, but as much as he wanted to air out his other clothes and render them wearable for the morrow, he didn't think it was proper to do so in front of a lady. He folded them neatly and returned them to the satchel instead.

When he emerged, clad in shirtsleeves and breeches once more, he found Charlie curled on the bed, her knees tucked to her chest and her hand slipped beneath her cheek. She wasn't even snoring.

He considered waking her so she could change into her nightgown but decided against it.

She'd matched his pace so readily, but the day must have been grueling for her to have fallen asleep so quickly. In fact, he felt near joining her. He could barely keep his eyes open. Gently, he removed her slippers and tucked them behind the screen next to his boots. He set his pack next to hers beside the door and returned to the bed. Tucking his arm around her, he held her close and lifted her to strip down the coverlets and sheets. She roused as he set her gently on the bed again.

"Anthony?" Her voice was gravelly with sleep.

"Sleep, love," he said softly. "I'll rouse you in the morning." He fought with the blankets, this time taking the thin sheet for himself and leaving her with the thicker coverlet.

As he draped it over her, she caught his wrist. "Aren't you coming to bed?"

Yes. He licked his lips. What harm would it do? He was far too tired to endanger her virtue tonight.

But tomorrow, after he had a full night's rest and woke to her pressed against him...

"No. I'll sleep on the floor. Get some rest."

There was only one pillow on the bed, so he rolled up his cloak and stretched out in the narrow space next to the bed. If she got up in the night, she might trip over him.

Fortunately, they both were too exhausted for further argument on the topic. Charlie fell asleep again without comment. If she snored, Gray didn't hear her. He slept that deeply.

* * *

WHEN HE NEXT WOKE, IT WAS TO A THROBBING head and Charlie's groan.

"My head... Anthony, where did you put the packs?"

"By the door." He winced as the sound of his voice renewed the pounding in his skull. When Charlie stirred in bed, he shut his eyes tight and held still as she stepped over him.

"Which door? I only see the one."

"That's the only bloody door in here." He wasn't proud of his descent into profanity, but Lord have mercy, his head hurt. He sat up, rubbing it.

"They aren't here. Are you sure you didn't set them behind the screen?"

What in the blazes? He rubbed his eyes and stared blearily at the empty spot near the door where he'd set down the packs. The room spun a bit.

Charlie danced from foot to foot. "Would you mind vacating the room? I need to use the chamber pot. Perhaps we left the packs downstairs. It might bear checking."

He accepted his boots from her and let her herd him from the room. Only once the door shut behind him did clarity return. He couldn't have left the packs in the dining room, for they'd needed them in order to change clothes last night. His stomach sinking like a stone, he ambled downstairs to check.

He found Stills seated at a table in front of a hearty breakfast of bacon and eggs.

"Captain." The lieutenant started to stand, but Gray waved him down.

"Have you seen Charlie's and my satchels?"

"You mean the ones you brought up with you last night?"

Gray swore at the confirmation.

Alarmed, Stills rose. His hand flew to the pistol on his belt as if he was ready to do battle. "What's the matter?"

"Our packs weren't in our room this morning." How could Gray have slept through an intruder? In fact, hadn't he locked the door? He couldn't recall. Shaking his head, he asked, "Where is yours?"

"With the horses."

They both bolted for the stables. Gray hoped to find all three packs safe and sound. Instead, all they found were the two skinny horses.

Gray cursed the air blue. The packs contained their clothes, their provisions, the bloody compass, even the bulk of his money. All he had left were the few coins he kept tucked into his boot in case of pick-pockets.

They'd been robbed.

19

*I*f not for his family name, Gray didn't know what he would have done. The few coins he had left would purchase a meal or perhaps a room, if he wasn't terribly picky about the state of the bed; it would not cover the two meals, room, and stabling at the ramshackle inn.

Fortunately, the innkeeper was so apologetic over the fact that Gray had been robbed blind that he had been convinced to settle the account with Gray's older brother, Morgan. Gray had scrawled a quick explanation and note of apology for this unforeseen expense to be delivered to his brother with the request for payment.

Unfortunately, they didn't have time to chase down the thieves or their belongings. Without a compass, Gray would have to rely on his wits and the directions he received. Since the innkeeper knew of his family, he asked the man directly for the shortest route to Tenwick Abbey. This time, Gray was taking no chances.

Then it made no sense, as they stopped at a fork in the road, that the same information Stills had gleaned from the innkeeper conflicted with what the man had told Gray.

"I'm certain he said to turn left," Stills said, his voice adamant. "I was very clear on where we meant to go; I even mentioned Locksley as the nearest town."

"I was also clear," Gray said, his voice tight. "He instructed me to turn right."

Had he misheard? *Blast*—he had been so meticulous to repeat the directions back, hoping to avoid such a mishap. *No, it must be Stills's error.*

"Sir, I'm afraid—"

"We will turn right." Gray's voice was final. Behind him, Charlie adjusted her hold. She didn't speak a word.

Stills's mouth flattened into a thin, mulish line. For a moment, Gray thought he might try to contradict him or stubbornly take the other path regardless. Gray handled the situation as he would have at sea. He squared his shoulders and stared down his longtime second-in-command. *I am the commanding officer.* Even if he didn't have a vessel to command, at present.

After a tense moment, the man capitulated. "Very well, sir. While we're stopped, would you mind if I used the bushes to p—" He glanced at Charlie and changed what he was about to say. "Relieve myself?"

Gray nodded. He dismounted to hold the reins of the other horse while Stills escaped into the tree cover. Charlie also slid off the horse in order to stretch her arms and legs.

"Would you like to make use of the bushes as well?"

She shook her head. "Thank you, but I'm fine."

He stifled a sigh and glanced up at the cloud-dotted sky.

Not long later, Stills emerged. They mounted and continued down the right path. Before ten minutes had passed, Stills's steed entered a frenzy.

The lieutenant struggled to remain on horseback as his mount reared, shrieking. Stills shouted, not helping to calm the horse at all. As the horse lowered onto all four legs, it shrieked again and bucked Stills out of the saddle. Charlie clutched Gray's middle as he shortened the reins, encouraging their mount to back away rather than get caught up in the calamity. The moment Stills landed on the ground, his arms curled around his head, Charlie loosened her hold.

"Oh dear." She slid from the horse's rump and skirted the edge of the path to see to Stills's welfare. As she knelt beside him, she gently touched his shoulder. "Lieutenant Stills, are you injured?"

Lud! Gray hoped not. He dismounted swiftly. He looped his steed's reins around a tree then slowly approached the other. It favored its right foreleg as it danced away. While Charlie tended to Stills, Gray cooed softly to the horse, trying to convince it that he wasn't a threat. If it bolted, it might trample Stills and Charlie in its panic.

The moment he succeeded in approaching the horse, he stroked the beast on the nose and tied the reins to a different tree, out of reach of his mount. When he ran his hand down the horse's front leg to examine the injured area, he found it hot to the touch. *Confound it!* He didn't know enough about equine injuries to be able to say for certain, but at his guess, the horse was now lame. It certainly wouldn't be able to bear a rider if it could barely bear its own weight.

What were they to do? His mother's life was in danger, and they'd gone from three horses to one.

His heart thrumming, he crossed to stand behind Charlie, who helped Stills to sit up. Gray clasped his hands behind his back, trying to bury his impatience over yet another delay in a long string of them. After all, his longtime companion might be hurt. If he was, the closest place to seek help was likely the town they'd passed an hour ago. An hour moving in the wrong direction, with a lame horse and a man who might not be able to keep his seat even if the horse could bear him, would not do.

A groan escaped Stills's lips as he tested his range of movement. "I'm all in one piece, Captain."

Gray stifled a sigh of relief. "It's more than I can say for the horse. It might be lame. It's certainly favoring its leg."

Charlie released Stills to sit under his own power, which he seemed perfectly capable of doing. She twisted to look up at Gray. "What does that mean?"

"It means we'll have to walk. If you're capable, Lieutenant. If not, we do have one more horse. You can ride mine while Miss Vale and I walk." It was unconscionable to ask a lady to walk when she could be astride, but Stills was injured, after all.

He grimaced as he stood. "I'm able to walk. I'll lead my horse, sir."

Nodding, Gray said, "Very well. Charlie?"

Scowling, she got to her feet and brushed off her

skirt. "I'm not an invalid. I'm capable of walking on my own. Lieutenant Stills is—"

"I said I am well, Miss Vale. Please take me at my word." Stiffly, Stills thrust his shoulders back and clasped his hands behind him.

"What happened?" Gray asked. This latest mishap didn't sit well with him. It was as though the universe were conspiring to assure that he didn't reach Mother in time.

"A garden snake on the path, sir. It must have spooked the horse. It's a stroke of bad luck that the horse became lame because of it."

A stroke of bad luck... or a purposeful design. If Stills hadn't been thrown from his horse, Gray might begin to suspect that *he* was behind these mishaps. After all, it couldn't be Charlie's fault—he made it his purpose to be her guardian throughout this trip. She never left his sight, save to use the bushes, and she was as driven to save his mother's life as he was.

Stills, on the other hand, had no such personal stake in the outcome of their mission. Why *had* he relinquished a command post so readily to follow Gray into the English wilderness?

"With the horse lame, we'll lose more time. We should waste as little of it as possible. Are you ready to continue?"

Stills nodded, solemn.

Gray herded Charlie toward the horse they shared. "I said I can walk," she protested loudly.

"We'll take turns," he promised, though he meant no such thing.

That seemed to placate her somewhat, at least long enough for him to corner her under the ruse of adjusting the stirrups.

Softly, he murmured, "Don't react if you can manage."

Her lips barely moved as she whispered back, "React to what?"

"To what I'm about to tell you. Do you find this latest mishap at all suspicious?"

Charlie stroked the horse's nose, pretending to pay him no mind. "The horse's panic, you mean?"

"The lame horse is eerily similar to what happened to your horse shortly after we set out. This after the good lieutenant seemed adamant to lead us in the wrong direction a second time." Although Gray didn't voice as much, he had to wonder if Stills had a hand in robbing them, as well.

Charlie's lower lip wobbled. She started to turn to look behind her, at Stills, but she visibly stopped herself. She held Gray's gaze instead. "You think he's sabotaging us?"

"I wonder if we would have made it to Tenwick Abbey already if he weren't here."

When he beckoned her forward, Charlie came complacently. She pressed her lips together as he gripped her by the waist and transferred her, sidesaddle, onto the horse. It would be awkward to ride like that, no doubt, given that they no longer had a sidesaddle to offer her, but with Gray leading the horse he hoped she would be able to keep her seat.

His hand lingered around her hips as he leaned close enough to add, "I don't know why he doesn't want us to reach Mother in time, but one thing is clear. We've an enemy in our midst."

By the time they reached the next rest point to water the horses, when Anthony had promised to speak more on his warning away from the possibility of Lieutenant Stills overhearing, Charlie's stomach was in knots. She tried to remain as serene and composed as Mama, but she feared she didn't do much good.

She laid her hands on Anthony's shoulders as he reached up to lift her down. However, the moment her toes touched the ground, her knees turned to jelly. She would have fallen if not for Anthony's support.

He adjusted his hold on her and used his solid body to keep her upright. "Steady. It's all right. I've got you."

Charlie tilted her face up to his, but when she tried to thank him, her voice fled toward her navel. They stood close enough for her to feel his breath fanning her hair.

Anthony raised his voice. "Stills? Could you take the horse? Miss Vale isn't accustomed to riding and needs my support for a moment."

"Of course, sir."

Charlie jumped at the nearness of his voice, that of an enemy, the man they'd traveled with, Anthony's second-in-command. She didn't want to believe it, not only because it made her heartbeat flutter with fear.

As Lieutenant Stills led away the horse, Anthony leaned closer to lean his forehead against hers. "Good thinking," he whispered. "We should have a few moments alone."

She hadn't feigned weakness. Unfortunately, weak knees seemed to be a byproduct of both riding the horse for a prolonged period of time and finding herself this close to Anthony. Nevertheless, she didn't confess as much, for fear that he didn't feel the same about her. Once again, he hadn't joined her in bed, even if she would have been far too exhausted to welcome his advances.

She tried to push her attraction to him out of her mind, as difficult as that sounded. They had a more important matter to discuss—one that might endanger their lives, if his suspicion was correct. She'd mulled it over for an hour or more while riding, and she couldn't refute his claims. He was right; these mishaps occurred far too frequently to be mere coincidences.

"What do we do?" she whispered, mere inches away from his mouth.

He traced her cheek as he tucked a strand of her hair behind her ear. With their belongings stolen, she hadn't had her hairbrush to render her locks neat. They stubbornly escaped any attempts to tame them by braiding.

After he darted a glance toward the potential traitor, currently guiding the horses to drink from the stream, Anthony whispered, "I don't know what we can do for the moment. He's armed."

Charlie fought the urge to roll her eyes. "As are you." She pointedly lowered her gaze to his belt, where a pistol and dirk resided.

It didn't look nearly as formidable as when he was clad in his full captain's uniform, but his waistcoat and coat had been stolen by the thieves, along with the rest of their belongings. Perhaps it had been her stroke of good luck that she'd fallen asleep with her clothes on rather than only her nightgown. Only the articles left behind the screen—boots and belt—had been overlooked. Even her reticule had been snatched while they were asleep, and she contemplated how she could have been so drowsy as to sleep through that.

It wasn't the first time this morning that she'd chided herself for the lapse. No doubt Anthony battled the same self-blame. However, they couldn't find the thieves, nor their belongings; they had to address this threat instead.

With a grimace, Anthony adjusted the cloak he'd used for a pillow over his shoulder to cover his weapons. "Even if I am armed, I have no ammunition —that was in the pack. If Stills was the man responsible for taking our belongings, he undoubtedly left himself the bullets and gunpowder necessary to defend himself." Hesitantly, Anthony stroked her cheek. "Besides, you aren't armed, and I'd fear too much for your safety to confront him now. Such a confrontation can be frightening."

Charlie arched her eyebrows. "Do you think I'll fall to pieces the moment the first accusation is thrown?"

His silence spoke volumes.

She gritted her teeth. "Anthony, I'm not a watering pot. I won't dissolve to tears at the first sign of danger. Surely we've been traveling together for long enough for you to realize that."

At the chastisement, one side of his mouth lifted in a half grin. "You've proved that, but you still amaze me with your resilience and pluck. Any other woman of my acquaintance would have reached her limit."

This time, she couldn't suppress a roll of her eyes. "Perhaps you've been acquainting yourself with the wrong women. Any woman related to you, for instance, would act exactly as I am. Lud, Lucy would probably attempt a coup here and now."

"I'm thankful you have more sense than her, then." His chest expanded as he drew in a deep breath. As Lieutenant Stills finished watering the horses and turned, Anthony angled his back toward him and lowered his head closer to Charlie's. His lips brushed against her cheek in a faint caress as he continued to speak. "We'll stop at the next inn we find. We'll confront him there."

Charlie pursed her lips. When she turned her head, the corner of her mouth brushed against Anthony's. Her breath hitched as she battled the ache to kiss him once more. "Are you certain it's wise to confront him out of turn? He might just deny the entire debacle."

Tucking another strand of hair behind her ear, Anthony whispered, "What do you propose? We can't let him continue to sabotage us. No more can we bring him with us—what if he poses a danger to Mother?"

Why was he touching her so intimately? Only last night, he'd opted to sleep on the floor again. He hadn't kissed her for days, and she feared she'd misinterpreted the inclination on his part. She swallowed hard. "I can't think properly when you touch me like that."

A wolfish smile spread across his face as he dropped his hand to her shoulder. He seemed inordinately pleased with himself. "Is that so?"

"It is. This hardly seems like the most appropriate time. Later, when we're alone... " Lud, what was she saying? Her cheeks heated.

His smile faded. He leaned his forehead against hers once more and whispered, "I hope to discourage Stills from eavesdropping by making it look as though we're having an intimate conversation."

"We *are* having an intimate conversation!"

"I meant of the sort he wouldn't want to overhear. The sort lovers have."

Charlie had never been privy to such a conversation, so she decided to let the subject drop, even though she thought all these delays were driving him mad. What would they be talking about so closely that wouldn't be fit for prying ears?

Anthony swallowed audibly. "We won't be able to stand like this forever. What is your idea?"

"We catch him in the act."

To her surprise, Anthony tilted his head and kissed her. Her knees weakened once more, and she leaned against his muscular frame, letting him take command of her body. After a brief melding of mouths, he lifted his head. She kept her face turned up, hoping for another. When he didn't offer it, she opened her eyes. His hazel eyes were warm, his mouth soft and in the very beginning of a smile.

"Was he looking at us?" she asked, her voice hoarse.

"I haven't the faintest." He traced her mouth with his thumb. "Forgive me, but I couldn't resist."

"There's nothing to forgive." She wished he'd do it more. Unfortunately, her courage fled, and she bit her lip as she returned to business. "You like my idea, then? If he thinks we're able to procure another horse, he'll try to stall us or stop us in some way. If we catch him while he's in the act of sabotage, he's more likely to tell us the truth."

Anthony nodded. "We'll do it in a village, prefer-

ably one big enough to have its own magistrate. I don't
have enough coin for a horse, though. I'm not even
certain I have enough to house us, if the innkeeper
won't be convinced to charge the lodging to my
brother."

"We must try," she told him. "It's our best chance
to end this without bloodshed."

"I agree, love," he whispered, stroking her chin.
"Will you ride the horse again, then? I know you'd like
to walk, but we can't risk Stills harming our last horse
in any way."

She narrowed her eyes. Was he telling the truth, or
was he only concocting the lie in the hopes of
convincing her to ride? Unfortunately, he made a
convincing point. "Very well, but once we've dealt
with this threat, we are sharing the horse equally."

Anthony nodded. "You have my word. Are
you ready?"

A flock of birds erupted in her stomach at the
thought of traveling all day with a man who might
mean them serious harm. Nevertheless, she main-
tained her composure and nodded. "Let's reach this
village as soon as may be."

20

*B*y the time they reached a village Anthony deemed large enough to spend the night in, he looked haggard. Charlie supposed she might as well, if she'd had to walk all day. Their pace had been slowed to accommodate the lame horse, which Anthony had been loath to leave at the side of the road to fend for itself.

The sunset painted the sky in a brilliant array of red and gold as Anthony led the horse through the neat village street toward the crossroads at its center. Buildings encircled a three-story edifice, the biggest in the village by far. The painted swinging sign depicted a mug of ale but had no words.

When Anthony helped her from the horse, he lingered, hands on her waist as he waited to see if she could hold herself upright. His palms splayed against her, warm.

"Can you stand?" he asked, his voice rough.

She nearly pretended weak knees, simply for the excuse to keep him near. If he kissed her, she wouldn't have to pretend. However, they weren't in a clearing in the middle of a deserted forest; they stood in the center of a populated village. Even if he claimed them as man and wife yet again—which they had already decided they must in order to be united against Lieutenant Stills whenever he made his move—kissing in public would be unseemly.

She mustered a shaky smile. "Yes, thank you." Her voice emerged breathless. Their kiss in the forest had been so tentative—sweet, almost, in comparison with their other two kisses. She couldn't help but feel as though something between them had changed.

However, as he stepped back, he gave no indication that he was as affected by their nearness. She stifled her disappointment as he announced his intention to bring the horses to the stable. This was also according to plan, a plan they'd hatched little by little as they stopped to rest and water the horses. Each time, he had remained near to her, caressing her cheek or toying with her hair. He hadn't kissed her again, however much she had hoped that he would. In fact, their conversations after the first had been entirely too brief, a few sentences at most.

While Anthony and Lieutenant Stills stabled the horses, where Anthony was to inquire of the stable hands whether they had any additional horses they could buy or trade for their lame mount, Charlie entered the inn. Anthony's part in the ruse would soon be set, when his inquiries alerted Lieutenant Stills to the notion that they had enough money to replace their mounts. While the potential traitor was thus occupied, it was Charlie's duty to uncover whether or not this town housed a magistrate who might be able to help them.

The common room of the inn was full, with people clustered around a woman who played a pianoforte and sang like an angel. The words were a bit rougher than one might find in a London drawing room, but her performance was nothing short of stirring. The rapt attention she drew from the customers, mostly male, meant that Charlie was able to slip up to the long counter lined with stools and catch the attention of the barkeeper.

"Hello, sir. Would I be able to let a room from you, or is the innkeeper around?"

The young man, a few years shy of Anthony's age

at her guess, gave her a ready smile. "That's my pa. I can help you, miss."

"Mrs.," she corrected. "Mrs. Graylocke. My husband and our friend are bringing the horses round to the stables at this moment."

Calling herself Mrs. Graylocke felt strange and yet liberating at the same time. The thrill she got from lying tingled through her as though she were the spy her mother was.

Here she was, taking on a new identity for the sake of her mission and learning information that would help the coup they planned. This after adventuring through the British countryside, which, much to her disappointment, looked much the same as the woods and pastures surrounding Tenwick Abbey. It wasn't nearly the exotic adventure she dreamed of, but the fact that she'd found herself mired in this situation with Anthony...

She swallowed and smiled once more. "I'm afraid we must beg special favor. Are you familiar with the Graylocke name? Perhaps Tenwick?"

"Of Tenwick Abbey? You're married to a duke's son?" He set down the silverware he'd been polishing and tugged on his forelock. "Are you some grand lady? You're pretty enough to be."

That had been the ambition of her family, when

she'd initially made her coming out, for Charlie's beauty to ensnare the heart of a lord so they no longer had to live with the deplorable Lord Harker. Although her older sister had thought herself plain, in the end it had been her beauty and wit to ensnare the heart of a lord. She was the true Mrs. Graylocke, not Charlie.

Charlie had never wanted that future for herself. Not bewitching a man with her beauty—as if that were her only amiable quality. And certainly not marriage. Not even... with Anthony.

Blast. Where he was concerned, she feared that she would relinquish her dreams of adventure. When he kissed her, that felt like an adventure in itself.

She bit her lip and told the barkeep, "I'm no lady. My husband is—"

Was Anthony a lord? She'd only ever heard him called Captain Graylocke. Wait... his younger brother, Gideon, was a lord, so Anthony must be as well. He didn't act like one. Then again, all the Graylockes were much humbler than the typical aristocratic family.

Charlie smiled and completed, "Captain Anthony Graylocke, the middle child." That sounded odd. Anthony was a war hero. Surely he should be known for something other than the fact that his father—and now brother—was a duke.

The young man smiled at her. "Well, I can see how

a pretty bit o' muslin like you caught his eye. You'll want two rooms, or three?"

Three? He must assume that Anthony, like most London lords, would want to sleep away from his wife. Then again, given the glint in the young man's eye, perhaps he was hoping to join her in bed himself. *Not bloody likely.* Charlie clasped her hands together so hard, her fingernails left crescent-shaped imprints in her skin. If Anthony had been here...

Remain calm. She was in public and would take care to remain that way. In the meantime, perhaps she could use the young man's interest in her appearance to her advantage.

She gave him what she hoped was a helpless look. "I'm so happy you recognize my husband's family, because you see, we were robbed in the last inn we stayed in. We have no belongings to speak of and little money. Would it be possible to send the accounts of our stay to Tenwick Abbey to have them paid? We'll take two rooms and two meals and be on our way with as little trouble as possible."

The young man frowned. "I'd have to ask my pa, but I don't see as how that would be a problem. Whenever a lord passes through, we usually send the bill that way."

Perhaps Anthony had been right to choose a larger

village than the others they'd passed along the way. Charlie wondered if a smaller inn would have been so accommodating.

"Thank you. And"—she leaned forward, lowering her voice—"who would we turn to in matters of law around here? We're so far from London, I'm not sure if I should hope for a magistrate."

The barkeep puffed up. "Not so far from London, madam. It's only a day and a half away. Perhaps you can make it there in one if you push hard."

If that were true, they weren't nearly as close to Tenwick Abbey as they'd hoped. Anthony's ancestral home resided two days' travel away from London. Should they alter their destination?

The man added, "And we do have a magistrate in town, as it so happens. Sir Walter. He lives not half an hour down the main road on the way to London."

Charlie smiled, this time with relief. They had an ally nearby after all, if Lieutenant Stills proved too much to handle. "Thank you," she said with feeling. "I'll be certain to tell my husband of this and learn what he'd like to do regarding the theft."

Or in this case, the suspected traitor.

She laid her hand on the counter. "Would you be able to talk to your father about those rooms? We're dreadfully tired, and I'm certain my husband will want to retire the moment he returns from the stables. We'll eat in the room as well, if possible."

"I'll ask straight away," the young man said as he backed away from her.

So far, her part in the plan had gone smashingly. Had Anthony's?

* * *

THE HOSTLER MADE A DISAPPROVING NOISE UNDER his breath as he examined the horse's foreleg. "You shouldn't have traveled with her so far," he admonished. "She needs time off that leg, more of it now that she's spent the day making that injury worse. It might have been healed in a week."

Although Gray had expected that pronouncement, it chafed nonetheless. He didn't have a day to spare, let alone a week. He stifled his irritation. "I'm afraid I'm in rather a hurry to be home to Tenwick Abbey. Do you know if there are some horses for trade or sale? If we can trade this one for a fresh horse, or purchase another, it would much speed along our journey."

Frowning, Stills stepped closer. A couple inches shorter than Gray, the lieutenant lowered his voice to such a degree that Gray had to lean his head closer.

"Sir, we've been robbed. We don't have the blunt

to purchase a new horse. I don't know how we're to let rooms for the night."

"I keep the bulk of my coin in my boot. An old habit, after I was pickpocketed one too many times. It's enough for one horse, maybe two if someone will trade in the injured nag. My family name should do to purchase us rooms for the night."

Gray voiced the lie in the same cavalier manner he might have answered before he'd started suspecting Stills of being his enemy. The pit of his belly was as hard as rock. He didn't want to believe it, even if the evidence suggested Stills was responsible for their setbacks. This was a man Gray had fought alongside, a man he had entrusted his life to on more than one occasion.

Now, as he studied his longtime companion, Gray couldn't help but wonder if the flash of disapproval across the other man's face was his imagination. He might have been seeing signs that weren't there.

The hostler, unaware of their exchange, waited for Lieutenant Stills to clasp his hands behind him and take a step back before he spoke again. He trained his gaze on Gray.

"The innkeeper might be persuaded to sell one of the bays." He pointed to the far corner. "They don't get much exercise, these days, as the family has little cause to travel. I can ask and perhaps spread the word around town."

"Do that," Gray answered decisively. "We'll need to leave not long after dawn tomorrow. I'll confer with you then on the decision. And see if anyone would be willing to frank the cost to my brother, the Duke of Tenwick." If he found someone willing to relinquish their horse on his word that his family would pay, he might be able to procure mounts for both him and Charlie, after all.

Turning, he left their mounts in the stable hand's care and strode to the inn. He hoped that he and Stills had dallied long enough for Charlie to make her inquiries.

His second-in-command fell into step behind him as they entered the inn. The whispered chatter paused a minute as the patrons swung their gaze toward him. As the son of a duke, Gray was accustomed to scrutiny. He kept the cloak around his shoulders to shield his state of undress beneath and strode for the blonde seated on a stool at the end of the bar. As he reached her, the woman at the pianoforte began to pluck at the keys and drew the attention of those gathered in a ring around her.

Gray bristled as he witnessed the young man behind the counter, of an age with his younger brother, lean forward and give Charlie a wink. She shifted in place. Was she flattered?

He smothered the hot feeling in his chest as he laid his hand on the small of her back. "Hello, darling," he said, his voice tight. "Did you manage to procure us rooms?" He didn't take his eyes off the young man making calf eyes at her.

Perhaps he had no right to be jealous, seeing as he hadn't done the honorable thing and offered for her hand. They'd been alone together. If anyone learned that they'd shared a room—never mind that he'd slept on the floor—her reputation would be ruined. He should ask her to marry him. It was the right thing to do.

So what was stopping him? When she turned her gaze up to him with a smile, his heart skipped a beat. She was too beautiful by half, wild and somehow lady-like at the same time.

She had the mettle to do whatever was necessary, and the strength of character not to fall to hysterics at the least setback. She might make him a very good wife —whether he would make her a good husband was hard to say. He'd been waiting for years for the wild streak in him to fade before he considered taking a wife. It hadn't yet, but if she was a bit wild at heart, too, maybe it didn't need to.

These questions, compounding upon the problem with his mother, made his head throb. He could only focus on one problem at a time. That had to be saving Mother's life.

The flirtatious barkeeper said, "I've checked with Pa. Your rooms are all squared away. Pa said you might have three rooms, if you'd prefer to sleep apart from your wife, my lord."

And have this bounder join her instead? Gray gritted his teeth. "Thank you, but I prefer to share a bed with my wife."

The young man's smile faded as Gray pinned him beneath the same hard stare he gave misfits who joined his crew. The man tugged on his forelock. "Of course, my lord. I can show you to your rooms, if you're ready."

"I am."

As he started after the innkeeper's son, Stills asked, "Might we arrange a private room to eat supper?"

Gray exchanged a look with Charlie. They'd agreed to keep their distance from Stills, not only because they feared their suspicions about him would come into the open if they spent too much time socializing.

Gray had never been particularly adept at subterfuge—unlike the rest of his family, it seemed. If they were going to catch Stills in the act of sabotage, he had to keep his distance.

Charlie feathered her hand over Gray's arm. "Didn't you promise to take supper with me... alone?" She licked her lips before speaking the last word.

Throughout the day, Stills had witnessed enough intimate moments between them, mostly concocted for the benefit of keeping their suspicions secret, for him to understand why they might want privacy. Nevertheless, he seemed disapproving as Gray answered in the affirmative.

"I did give her my word. We should all turn in early, as well. It's been a long day, and we'll be riding hard if I can find us another horse or two."

Stills didn't say a word, but Charlie beamed as she took his arm and strolled with him. "That sounds like a grand idea!"

Raising his voice, Gray asked the barkeep, "Would you be able to arrange for our meals to be sent up to our rooms?"

"Of course, my lord."

As they reached the base of the stairs, Stills smiled. "Then I suppose I'll see you both at dawn." If Gray hadn't suspected him to be the orchestrator of their recent mishaps, he would have thought the warmth in his voice to be genuine.

In contrast, his answering smile felt brittle. "That we will."

He guided Charlie up the steps to the second story, where the barkeep directed them to two rooms. When the young man held the door open for Charlie to enter, Gray caught and held his gaze. He stepped in after her and thanked the barkeeper curtly. He planted himself between the young man and Charlie until the door shut.

If she noticed his jealous behavior, she ignored it. When he turned, he found her perched on the coverlet of the bed. The quilted bedspread was of much finer quality than the last two inns at which they had stayed the night. The bed and, indeed, the room as well were larger and furnished to better suit a ducal son. Not that it mattered a whit to him, but the innkeeper must have allotted the nicest room to him and Charlie, if the intricately painted screen and carved wooden vanity were any indication.

Charlie toed off her slippers, leaving them at the foot of the bed as she drew her knees to her chest. "Now what do we do?"

He crossed to the window, opening the shutters to allow a good view of the courtyard below.

At the corner of his field of vision resided the stables, likely better visible from Charlie's vantage on the bed. He sat next to her, bracing his palms on the bedspread to avoid the temptation of touching her. Whether Stills attempted to enter their room or abscond with their horses, Gray would be ready for him.

"Stills won't make a move until there is certain to be no witnesses about. We'll wait until the noise dies down below. Then we'll have to be on our guard."

GRAY DIDN'T KNOW PRECISELY WHEN HE DOZED off, but he woke as Charlie shifted her head beneath his cheek. Her soft hair brushed his skin. If his back and neck didn't ache so much from the prolonged position, he might have considered it a perfectly pleasant way to wake up.

"Anthony, do you see that?" She spoke in a whisper, barely disturbing the silence.

He blinked hard. With all light doused in the room, his eyes adjusted rapidly to the meager moonlight drifting out of the cloud-dotted night sky. As he squinted out the window, a flicker of light danced behind a darker shadow, silhouetting a hunched figure.

Panic doused him. He shot to his feet with alacrity. "Stills." *Blast.* He regretted falling asleep. By the time they reached the ground floor, the man might have already done away with the horses. "Stay here. Or better yet, fetch the magistrate so we have him on hand."

Charlie stood, crossing her arms. "The devil I will! I'm going with you. I won't leave you to face a traitor alone."

If Stills hurt her, Gray would never forgive himself. He'd promised her parents that he would keep her safe. Even more, he'd promised himself. However, if Stills somehow got the upper hand... He didn't have time to scrutinize his options. Time was of the essence.

Reluctantly, Gray capitulated. "Very well. Please, Charlie, I'm trusting you not to put yourself in undue danger. If this turns physical, let me handle him."

"Hand me your pistol."

He frowned. "I beg your pardon?"

She held out her hand, asking again for the useless weapon. "Your pistol."

"I haven't got any ammunition."

"No, but Stills might not know that. I can use it to bluff, or at the very least, I can club him over the head with it if he gets too close."

As he handed over the weapon, Gray silently vowed not to allow the enemy close enough for her to make good on her promise. "Hurry. We don't have much time."

She didn't argue but donned her slippers as she followed in his footsteps. He kept one hand on the hilt of his dirk, his only weapon if this came to blows. Gray hoped to find his former second-in-command in such a compromising position that the man would have no choice but to surrender to his fate. Honorably, as was done when they took prisoners of war.

Their footfalls on the wooden floorboards provided the only sound as they barreled down to the nearest exit. As he fumbled for the latch, he held up his hand to advise caution. Charlie didn't protest, so he eased the door open.

Dew or recent drizzle glinted off the scattered weed sprouting near the wall. The packed earth was soft, not quite mud as he stepped into the courtyard. The stable loomed ahead, with the glow of the lantern out of sight. Had Stills already left, or had he heard their approach and lain in wait? Cautiously, Gray eased forward, keeping himself between the stables and Charlie as he eased along the wall of the inn. He breathed shallowly. The air was damp, with a bit of an acrid bite.

Charlie ghosted her hand over his shoulder. "Do you smell smoke?"

He cursed viciously. What had Stills lit on fire—the stables or the inn? He bolted for the stables, drawing his dirk as he dashed.

Stills crouched on the far side, muttering about the dampness of the grass as he tried to light the stable wall on fire using the lantern. Smoke curled, from here and elsewhere, given the increased bite to the air. The moment he glanced up to see Gray's approach, Gray charged.

He slammed Stills into the wall. As the lantern toppled onto the damp grass and snuffed out, it left spots of light on his vision. Blind, he grappled with Stills for the dirk still in his hand. Instinct warred with years of memories. The man was his comrade in arms… or so Gray had thought. He wanted to avoid bloodshed if he could.

The dirk slipped out of his sweaty palm and onto the ground. He wrestled with Stills, who grunted as he groped for the weapons on his waist. Gray slammed him into the wall again to knock the breath from his opponent. An elbow in his ribs did the same to him.

"Cease your struggles, or I'll shoot!"

Bloody hell, Charlie! What was she thinking? Her pronouncement didn't deter Stills in the least.

Voice strained with effort as he continued to fight

Gray, the traitor bit off, "You wouldn't risk shooting your lover."

Lover. Gray's stomach flipped at the word. Seemingly, they'd done an admirable job of convincing the enemy that they were intimately involved. If Stills got free, he could harm her. Gray fought harder, using his bulk to pin the slightly smaller man.

Heedless to the danger—or perhaps putting more faith in Gray's abilities than she ought, given his precarious hold—Charlie shortened the distance between them until she angled the pistol from a mere foot away. "From here, I cannot miss."

"You're bluffing," Stills said, even as he froze in place. "You don't have ammunition."

Gray tightened his hold painfully. "We procured some tonight." The lie tasted like cold steel on his tongue.

Sweat trickled down his neck. *Back away, Charlie,* he silently begged. The darkness likely prevented her from reading his expression, even though his eyes were starting to adjust once more.

"Surrender," Gray commanded.

A sneer entered Stills's voice. "I don't recognize your authority. I've never been loyal to you."

Gray fisted his hand in the man's shirt and hauled him away from the stable wall. He kicked the back of his knees, forcing him to kneel as he wrestled the traitor's arms behind him.

"Charlie, keep the gun trained on him, and divest him of his belt."

She did as he asked, her movements quick and jerky as she stripped the traitor of his weapons. At Gray's behest, she passed him the leather belt, which he used to bind Stills's hands behind his back before he searched the man for additional weapons. He found ammunition, a smaller pistol, and a sharp knife. He stamped out the wisps of smoke against the stables during the short search. Once he had the matter under control, he stood and placed himself between Stills and Charlie.

"You've been my second-in-command for years."

"Quite so," the traitor spat. "Years of my life wasted. And for what, to keep an eye on the correspondence your brother sent? He never sent you any sensitive material. Never so much as anything in code."

Charlie stepped abreast of Gray. "You're a French spy. You've been sabotaging our efforts all along."

Stills issued a low, mirthless chuckle. "It took you long enough to catch on. I'd say that was a compliment to my skills, but it's been pitifully easy to keep you off course."

"I trusted you," Gray said, his voice hard. Beneath

the surface, his conviction wavered. How could his closest comrade have been a French spy? He would have known. It couldn't be true.

"And now we'll finally get our revenge when your mother gets what she deserves."

Gray's ears rang. When they and his vision cleared, he'd pinned Stills to the stable wall by his throat. The wood still trembled from the force of the blow. "What do you know of the plot?"

Stills gasped for breath around Gray's hand. Disgusted, Gray recoiled and dropped his arm.

After several deep breaths, the spy croaked, "Nothing. However, I knew when I heard of the plot that this was my chance to make a difference in the war. You'll never make it in time after all I've done."

Gray's heart dropped into the soles of his boots. *It can't be.* They would save Mother yet. They had to.

Charlie laid a hand on his arm. Her touch soothed him. "He's wrong," she said softly. "What has he done? So we're a bit closer to London than we aimed to be. Morgan's child is not yet four months old. Lady Graylocke will be at Tenwick Abbey with her grandson, I'm sure of it. She's safe."

She was safe, unless the assassin sought her out there. The information had boasted that the French wanted to prove they could touch the British spymaster anywhere, even among friends. *What more intimate a place than with her family? Dear Lord, were Morgan and his child in jeopardy as well?* Gray felt sick.

Charlie added, "Causing our horses to fall lame and steering us in the wrong direction will not stop us, Anthony. We will stop this plot."

When Stills started to speak, he coughed instead. The sound was raw. After spitting to the side, he managed to force out his words. "You think that's all I've done. Then you're still blind. I was the person who dampened the map and steered us into the embankment. Ensuring the horses threw a shoe or fell lame, leading us down the wrong path—it was too simple to be truly satisfying. Not to mention, you two were pitifully easy to drug the night I stole your belongings to keep us off track. Even now, you're far too busy contending with me to put out the fire at the other end of the stables."

Confound it! He'd thought there was too much smoke for that one tiny fire. "Stay here and keep him under watch," he commanded Charlie, hoping Stills was too trussed up to do her any harm. "I'll save the horses."

After all, they had no hope of reaching his mother in time if they didn't have mounts.

21

*C*harlie's ears still rang with cries of *"Fire!"* hours afterward. Anthony's dirk rested across her knees, in case Stills lunged toward her. She aimed the empty pistol at him to keep him in line. Her arms ached from switching the pistol back and forth for nearly two hours.

The fire hadn't grown large enough to cause a debilitating amount of damage to the stable. With the recent rain, the wood had been sufficiently damp to ward away the flames. However, the smoke was another matter. The building still hadn't cleared of it to the satisfaction of the lead hostler. Given the way he hovered over each of the mount's heads in turn, he worried over their continued health. A local physician examined those brave enough to have plunged into the smoky building to help.

While shouting a warning to rouse the innkeeper and his employees, Anthony had been the very first of that number. Despite his bravery, he'd waved away the physician's attention in order to ensconce himself in a tête-à-tête with Sir Walter, the magistrate who had recently arrived. How long did it take for him to explain their situation—and their captive—to the older man?

"He doesn't love you, no matter how he pretends."

Cursing her inattention, Charlie turned her back on the conversation between Anthony and the magistrate. She fixed her gaze and her aim on Lieutenant Stills once more but didn't respond.

"He's a seaman, desperate for female company. The only thing he's interested in resides beneath your skirts."

Charlie gritted her teeth. "Don't be crass."

"Don't be a fool. He isn't the honorable man he pretends to be."

You're wrong. Charlie knew that for a fact. This would be the third night they would share a room. The last several times she'd invited him into bed with her, he'd declined and slept on the hard, uncomfortable floor. She expected no different tonight.

Anthony arrived, cutting the conversation short. Two bullish men, one with a squashed nose and the other carrying a lantern, accompanied him and Sir Walter. As they reached Charlie, Anthony offered his hand. She accepted his help to stand, her legs a bit stiff from sitting in one position for so long. Sir Walter's men took Lieutenant Stills in hand.

The moment Charlie was on her feet, Anthony introduced her to the magistrate and thanked the man for his aid in taking charge of Lieutenant Stills.

Something about the way Anthony clipped off his words told her that he was not pleased with the outcome of this night. Charlie wondered whether it was because his closest friend had been unmasked as the enemy, or because Anthony would rather turn him over to his superiors than a country magistrate. Charlie rankled over not being able to present an enemy spy to Lord Strickland, who could extract better information than their efforts had yielded. However, they didn't have the time or the resources to transport a prisoner themselves. They had to trust in the local branch of the law to see that justice was served.

"Forgive us," Anthony said as he clasped her elbow. "It's been a dreadfully long night, and we must depart early on the morrow."

Their mission was far from over, but as Anthony steered her into the inn and up the stairs to their shared room, Charlie's heart pounded with excitement. She didn't know how she would possibly sleep.

Together, they had captured a French spy. Perhaps she hadn't played as big a role in the capture as she would have liked, seeing as the altercation had turned physical, but she preferred to think that her bluff had turned the tide of the fight. It certainly seemed to have been enough to keep Lieutenant Stills in line while she awaited the magistrate's men. Now that they had dealt with that unexpected threat, they would be able to reach Tenwick Abbey without issue. After all, Anthony had doused the fire long before it had reached the horses.

As they reached the corridor above, Anthony dropped his palm to cradle the small of her back. The intimate touch roused a shiver up her spine. Fighting against knees that threatened to turn to jelly, she entered their room and waited for him to follow and shut the door. The moment he did, he leaned his back against it.

Had Lieutenant Stills been right in warning her that Anthony cared for no more than her body? Charlie had encountered many a man who dismissed every part of her save for her beauty. Anthony, however, did not. If he hadn't thought her capable and strong, he would never have left her alone with a dangerous spy, even one that had been defeated.

However, at that moment, Charlie craved a bit of physical admiration. The gentle kiss he'd given her earlier that day seemed like ages ago. They were together, alone, and he had the opportunity to prove his former second-in-command correct and ravage her. The thin light wafting in from the open window made his eyes gleam with promise.

"Why don't you strip out of your gown? It must be damp after sitting on the grass for so long. I promise not to look."

That blasted honorable man. Lieutenant Stills's pronouncement was nothing more than hogwash. Charlie stifled a sigh and retreated behind the dressing screen to doff her muslin dress and slippers. She removed her stays for comfort. When she emerged again, Anthony had lit a candle and removed his boots. He stood by the vanity, facing the wall.

Since he appeared good to his word and wouldn't peek at her state of undress, she crossed and laid her clothing over the vanity to dry for tomorrow's travel. As she straightened, she brushed against him. Awareness of him raised the hairs on her arms.

His shoulders swelled as he took a breath. She licked her lips as she beheld him. Clad in only his shirtsleeves, his muscles rippled beneath the cloth. Unable to resist, she reached out to touch him.

His held breath turned into a groan. "Go to bed, Charlie."

I will, if you'll join me. She wasn't quite that brazen. She swallowed hard before whispering, "Earlier today, you said you kissed me because you couldn't resist."

He half-turned but didn't lower his gaze from hers. For a moment, he did nothing more than look at her, as if he waged an inner war. "I couldn't resist."

"Perhaps I wish you wouldn't try."

"Charlie, we are—"

"Alone. I know." She doubted that was what he meant to say, but she didn't want to hear him hide behind an excuse. Certainly not the mission they shared.

His eyes darkened as his gaze swept downward for the briefest of moments. Color warmed her cheeks at the notion of him seeing her in nothing but her chemise, but she didn't attempt to cover herself. It would have been in vain, in any case.

She cupped his cheek, her palm scraping against three days of unshaved stubble. "This time, perhaps I'm the one who cannot resist." Stepping closer, she rose on tiptoe to kiss him.

The moment her lips touched his, his mouth softened. She wrapped her arms around his shoulders, as much for balance as anything else. After a moment's hesitation, he embraced her just as close.

He tried to end with that quick, chaste kiss, but Charlie wasn't ready to part from him. She nipped at his lower lip, demanding more. With a groan, he cupped the back of her head and gave it to her.

Sensation flooded her as she surrendered to the kiss. He pressed her intimately against him. A moment later, he slipped his hand beneath her bottom and lifted her. Her chemise, which ended just below the knee, rose higher over her thigh as she wrapped her legs around him to keep from falling.

Her world teetered, and next she knew, her back pressed against the mattress. Anthony continued to kiss her, resting the bulk of his weight on one forearm. As he traced the contours of her figure, she melted against him, ready to follow his lead.

Unfortunately, it ended too soon. As he reached the dip in her waist, he stiffened and drew himself away. He grabbed one of the pillows off the bed and held it between them as he rose.

"Anthony?"

"Goodnight, Charlie." His voice was gravelly as he

retreated to the vanity. "Keep the coverlet. I'll use my cloak."

He intended to sleep on the floor again. She stifled a sigh. As she sat up, her body still awakened from his touch, she wrapped her arms around her waist. "It wouldn't kill you to sleep next to me, you know."

He didn't answer as he stretched out on the floor with his back to her and his cloak pulled up over his shoulder.

Charlie bit the inside of her cheek as she blew out the candle and slipped between the sheets. Anthony was far too honorable. Perhaps he didn't love her, but it was clear that he would never take advantage of their predicament.

Staring at the ceiling, she waited for exhaustion to retake her after these long few days. Her heart continued to pound as she thought of Anthony instead.

If she wanted something from him, it appeared that she would have to take it herself.

STORM CLOUDS BREWED TO THE WEST, THICK froths of darkness churning the air kicked up by the horse's hooves. The air smelled thick with the promise of rain. Charlie's arms tightened around Gray's waist, a sure sign that she noticed the impending storm, too.

Blast! If only they'd had a second horse, they might have made better time. However, as grateful as the innkeeper was for their assistance in saving his stables and apprehending the man responsible for lighting it on fire, he'd had only one horse to offer them in their journey.

The others had been too affected by the smoke to serve as reliable mounts. Therefore, he and Charlie yet again rode two to a horse, necessitating frequent stops and a pace no greater than the occasional trot.

"We won't make it to Tenwick Abbey," Charlie shouted above the mounting wind.

Considering that evening would be upon them in an hour or two and they'd yet to halve the distance, Gray had to agree with her pronouncement. However, it didn't sit well with him—it was possible that Stills had been successful in delaying them too long.

He dug his heels into the mount's side, urging the horse to a quick trot despite the prolonged pace of the day and heavier-than-average load.

"If we don't find shelter, we'll be caught in the storm."

At the mouth of an offshoot of the road, Gray halted and twisted in the saddle to try to meet Charlie's gaze. He was only moderately successful. The clouds behind them blotted out the sun, deepening the afternoon gloom until it seemed closer to twilight. The overhanging branches of an unusual, L-shaped tree further dampened his field of vision.

"What do you suggest?" he asked. He had to raise his voice in order to hear it. A gust of wind blew strands of Charlie's hair into his face. "I can find a hollow and make a lee to shelter us, or we can stop at the next farmhouse we see."

Charlie pointed toward the tree. "I recognize that tree. We're near to Lucy's country estate. When I left with Mama, she was in residence there. It must be no more than an hour's ride away."

Gray judged the looming clouds then glanced down the path. Did they have an hour before the storm was upon them? The faint rumble in the distance didn't bode well.

"Are you certain this is the route to Lucy's estate?" With his sister's recent marriage, Charlie couldn't have been there often, and certainly not from this direction.

"I couldn't mistake that tree. Lucy called it provenance that her initial was already marking the route."

Gray chuckled under his breath and shook his head. "You mean to say she didn't prune the tree to look that way?"

"I'm afraid not. It grew in that shape of its own volition."

Another, louder rumble growled behind them like a savage beast. They didn't have a moment to waste.

"Hold tight, then. We must make haste."

He kicked the horse into a canter as Charlie tightened her hold around his waist.

By the time Charlie tapped on his shoulder and pointed at the path twining up to a grand manor, they were both soaked to the skin. Gray had insisted she take his cloak, but with the way the wind whipped the rain into them, it didn't do much good. His shirt was plastered to his back with moisture, and Charlie had been pressed tight against it for the past hour.

"That's it," Charlie yelled.

As another crack of thunder split the air, Gray scarcely heard. His ears rang as he turned the agitated horse down the winding path. The sky lit up with a flash of lightning that blanketed the horizon from end to end. It left a purplish imprint on his vision as it disappeared.

The ground churned beneath the horse's hooves as they battled down the drive toward the stables. The doors were shut tight, but Gray prayed someone was left in attendance to see to their mount. The poor beast heaved with pants, from either exhaustion or fright.

Charlie jumped and tightened her hold on him as another peal of thunder shook the air. "Almost there," he promised. He couldn't hear his own voice above the wind.

The moment they skidded to a halt in front of the stables, Gray dismounted and lifted Charlie to her feet. For a moment, her legs trembled, and she leaned against him. At any other time, he would welcome the excuse to hold her. Now, unfortunately, he feared they might catch their death.

He pointed to the manse and ordered her to rouse Lucy and explain the situation. He didn't know if she heard his words, but she dashed toward the manor nonetheless.

He walloped on the stable door. After a moment, it opened a crack, fighting against the wind. He dug his fingers into the slit and pried it apart far enough to face a young stable boy. Over the roar of the wind and thunder, he explained that he was Lucy's brother and needed a place to stable his horse. The moment he turned over the steed, he bolted for the manor.

Charlie stood just inside the foyer, shivering and dancing from foot to foot in a widening pool of water.

She looked as pale as a ghost as she clutched his cloak to her tightly. Only one person, an aged and stoic man who likely served the household as either a footman or butler, occupied the room.

"Where's Lucy?"

"He sent a man t-t-to rouse her." Her teeth chattered.

Hell and damnation. She would fall ill if she didn't get out of those clothes soon. Unfortunately, he had no warmth to offer her but that of his own body. Although he was just as wet as she, he wrapped his arms around her and held her close. Her shivers abated as she burrowed against his chest.

When he heard footsteps, he reluctantly drew away. Clad in a flower-printed wrapper, Lucy barreled into the entry. A tall, auburn-haired man in a banyan followed on her heels. The moment she spotted her visitors, Lucy stopped short and clapped her hand over her mouth. "Anthony?"

It was lucky he had released Charlie, because in the next instant, he found his arms full of Lucy. She squeezed the life out of him. He returned the hug gingerly, his ears ringing from her babbling.

"How did you get here? Shouldn't you be at sea? Why are you with Charlie? Where are your things?"

Relief swept over him. If something had already

happened to Mother, Lucy would surely have mentioned it. Instead, she seemed her usual curious self, if not a bit glowy. Gray glanced at the man beside her, her husband, and decided he didn't like thinking about his little sister married, or what this new husband had to do with her glowing. Best not to mention their mission right away. He didn't want to upset Lucy, and since it appeared that nothing had happened to Mother yet, he'd ease into it.

He pulled back long enough to say, "It's a long story, and it's been a long journey." He frowned as he took in her attire once more. "Why are you dressed for bed? It can't yet be past suppertime."

Lucy turned as pink as a berry. "It's so dreadful outside, Alex and I thought we'd go to bed early."

Lud. He'd forget he'd asked. It seemed the fellow would get his heir sooner rather than later, at this rate. *No*—Gray didn't want to consider it when his own sister was the wife.

She turned from him to Charlie. "Dear me, you're both soaked to the skin. We have to get you both out of those clothes at once. Did you leave your valises at the stables?"

"We have no valises," Charlie answered. "We were robbed along the way."

Lucy looked horrified. Before she launched another barrage of questions, Gray held up his hand.

"Like I said, it's been a long and eventful journey."

"So it seems." Lucy insinuated herself between him and Charlie and guided them farther into the house. Their shoes squelched on the floor, but she didn't appear to notice. "Come, you can both have a hot bath and borrow some clothes from Alex and me. After that, I must hear everything."

22

*G*ray wanted nothing more than to see to his mother's safety, but since there was a storm raging, he knew she would not be in any public place. So she was safe for the moment.

After a hot bath and a proper change of clothes, Gray felt like a new man. Even if the clothes didn't fit as well as his own, the feel of the soft, clean cloth against his skin was heavenly. The chill of the rain was warded away by the crackling fire in the library hearth. It cast a rosy glow over the couple ensconced in the loveseat. Lucy leaned into her husband's embrace, more content than Gray had ever seen her. For her sake, he tried to relax and give Alex Brackley the benefit of the doubt.

Nevertheless, the moment he found himself alone with the man, he was going to set him straight. Gray would have preferred for Lucy to find herself a staid, bookish man who shared her academic interests, rather than a notorious rake.

If he'd been at home, he might have been able to prevent the match, and he wondered why Morgan had allowed it. Given the fond looks and affectionate touches they gave one another, his interference would not be appreciated. However, since Lucy had settled on a man infamous for entertaining multiple women, Gray needed to ensure that his attention wouldn't stray from his wife. Gray didn't care a whit if most noblemen kept mistresses; Brackley would not.

"So you happened upon her by chance?"

Gray grounded himself in the present as he laughed and continued his tale. "I did. She was trying to hold off a French invader with a letter opener. I'd never..."

He trailed off as a shadow entered the doorway. *Charlie.* He stood, admiring the way the borrowed periwinkle dress molded to her figure. Her hair was still damp but pinned to the back of her head with only two strands left free to frame her face. When she saw him, she smiled. He couldn't help but smile back.

"Never?" Lucy prompted.

His cheeks warming, he recalled that he and Charlie weren't alone. As much as he craved holding her close the way Brackley did Lucy, Gray held himself in check. It would be unseemly. Instead, he answered as Charlie crossed the room to sit in a vacant armchair. "I'd never seen anything like it. She was barbaric."

Charlie's smile grew. "Oh, are you telling them of the time you interfered where you weren't needed?" Her voice was falsely sweet, at odds with the challenging glint in her eye.

"I came just in time! He would have shot you, had I tarried but a moment."

He waited for her to settle into the chair before he resumed his seat. Lucy and her husband exchanged a smile as the long, winding tale continued.

Charlie and Gray took turns in the telling. She held no sensitive information back from the couple and divulged her purpose and the results of their secretive mission. Once they completed the winding tale of how they'd captured his second-in-command in the act of sabotage, Gray ended by saying, "As soon as the storm passes, we mean to be on our way to Tenwick Abbey. If you have a horse to spare to speed our journey, we would be grateful. We must warn Mother at once."

Lucy sat straighter. "Of course, we must. But she

isn't at Tenwick Abbey. After you departed, Charlie, she returned to the London townhouse."

No. Gray's heart skipped a beat. There were so many more opportunities for danger in London. *Damn and blast, what if it was already too late?* "Are you certain?"

"I am. She wrote me a letter asking me to join her, but I declined."

Gray got to his feet. Storm or no storm, he couldn't idle here if his mother's life was in jeopardy. "Then I'm afraid I must depart at once. We haven't a moment to lose."

Brackley also stood, his expression hard. "Quite right. Monsieur V tore apart my family. I cannot sit by and watch him do the same to yours."

Scowling, Lucy got to her feet with arms raised. "Sit down, both of you. There's nothing to be done in this storm."

"It's only rain," Gray said, even though he knew the danger to be much worse than he made it out to be. Lightning and thunder could spook the horse, if it didn't strike him. Low visibility meant a danger on the road, which in this torrent would be as substantial as soup. And of course, there would be the danger to his health if he remained out in the cold rain overnight.

Lucy glared at him. "I won't see either of you

madmen risking your lives by galloping off tonight. When the storm passes in the morning, we'll head out at first light."

"But Mother—"

"She'll survive the night. Didn't you say the assassin meant to strike her during an engagement among friends? She cannot leave the house in a storm like this, no more than you."

She was right. The storm had raged here for hours. It must have reached London by now and would keep Mother confined indoors for the duration. Her evening entertainments would have to be canceled.

Knowing that didn't make waiting any easier. He chafed at yet another delay, this one beyond anyone's power to halt. Charlie brushed his arm, a delicate touch that drew his attention to her. As she nibbled on her lower lip, his attention fastened to her mouth. *Confound it,* he thought, wondering why had they found themselves so close to family. The bath and change of clothes wasn't worth having to relinquish the freedom to kiss her.

When he cleared his throat, she hastily retracted her hand. "Why don't we have a hot meal and rest? We can push for London on the morrow. If we ride fast and change horses, we might be able to make it before nightfall."

It would be a punishing pace, one he didn't care to subject her to, but with his mother's life at stake, he didn't argue with her. They would both move heaven and earth to ensure that Mother's would-be assassin was arrested in time.

Her stomach gurgled, rousing a blush in her cheeks. "I'm starved," she confessed.

They'd pushed on rather than search out an eatery to break their fast. Although the innkeeper had provided them with vittles for their journey, Gray had barely nibbled on his, and Charlie hadn't eaten much more. His appetite had shriveled with every new delay in reaching Mother.

He offered his arm to her with a smile. "Let's eat then, my—" He cut himself off before he called her *dear*. "Friend." He fought not to make a face at his hasty choice of words. Blast, his feelings for her must be as clear as day.

The corners of her mouth trembled as she pressed her lips together. She looked to be fighting off a laugh as she laid her hand on his arm once more. "Yes, let's."

Attempting to ignore his sister's knowing look, he followed the lord and lady of the house to the dining room. Although he tried to focus on Charlie and the meal, he couldn't help but combat a growing knot of foreboding in his stomach.

What if they didn't reach Mother in time?

As Anthony set down his tumbler, still containing a lick of brandy, and made his excuses, Charlie's stomach tightened. He was worried. She could tell by the look and tightness of his eyes, belying his smile and claims of weariness.

She worried about Lady Graylocke as well, but she'd hoped that being among family would have allowed Anthony to relax for the evening.

They'd pushed themselves so hard these past couple of days that she feared he might have one foot in the grave if they kept this up. Although she refused to complain, she felt as translucent as mist. She had to believe that they would reach London and Lady Graylocke in time to avert the disaster. She didn't want to contemplate what might happen otherwise.

He caught her gaze. For a moment, he looked as though he wanted to say something profound, perhaps even ask to walk her to her door. After a hesitant pause, he said, "Goodnight, Miss Vale."

She smirked. Did he think he was being discreet? His family never stood on formality. "Goodnight, Captain Graylocke."

He held her gaze a moment longer before he left.

The moment his shadow whisked out of sight into the corridor, Lucy adjusted her position in the curve of her husband's arm. A gleam lit her eye. "How long have you two been courting?"

Charlie fought the urge to lick her lips. "I don't know if I'd call it courting. We've... grown close over the past couple days."

A sly smile curved Lucy's lips. "I bet you have."

Charlie fought off a blush. Lucy's tone brought to mind intimacies that Charlie hadn't shared with Anthony.

Lucy added, "Did you have separate rooms at the inn?"

Her husband tightened his hold around her shoulders. "Don't pry. I'm sure you wouldn't have looked fondly on Charlie had she attempted to learn the intimate details of our courtship."

"Why not? I told her everything. We keep no secrets."

Since that statement seemed to render him speechless—and perhaps a bit alarmed—Charlie took advantage of the moment to say, "If you know your brother at all, you'll know he was a perfect gentleman. He slept on the floor."

Lucy appeared disappointed at the answer. At least she seemed to believe Charlie.

Meanwhile, her husband didn't appear to be paying any attention to Charlie at all. He choked out, "Just what did you tell her?"

Lucy twisted in his arms to offer him a sweet smile. "All of it."

Oh dear. Was the notorious rake blushing? Charlie hid a smile behind her hand.

"I thought you promised not to write about the intimate details of our life."

"I didn't write about it. I told it verbally to Charlie. She's like a sister to me, Alex."

A warmth bloomed in Charlie's chest until Lucy added, "And soon I hope she'll be a sister in truth." She pinned Charlie beneath her stare. "I knew precisely how honorable my brother is. If indeed he did sleep in the same room as you, he'll make an offer for you. I'm certain."

An offer of marriage born of honorable instinct? How... boring. Charlie swallowed hard. "You know I don't mean to marry quite yet."

"So you'll break my brother's heart?" Lucy's mouth puckered.

Charlie rubbed her temple. "You just said he would only propose out of honor."

The dark-haired woman narrowed her eyes. Although her eyes were a deeper brown than Anthony's, the family resemblance between them was never plainer than when she looked suspicious.

"Has he kissed you?"

"Once or twice." More than that, but Charlie held her tongue.

"Then there is some affection between you."

She didn't know whether she would call those kisses affectionate. The way he looked at her sometimes, perhaps. But most of the kisses they'd shared had been wild.

Lord Brackley must have picked up on her unease, because he squeezed Lucy's shoulders. "Perhaps the inclination between them is something best left for them to decide, darling."

"But she must decide," Lucy insisted.

"We're in the midst of a mission," Charlie protested, her voice weak.

Lucy's voice lacked no conviction. "So were we. And soon that mission will be complete. What will you tell him then?"

He hasn't asked anything. Although he'd gotten freer with his kisses, he hadn't given her any indication that he wanted more.

"Think about it," Lucy insisted.

Charlie forced a smile as she stood. It felt brittle. "I will. I fear it's been a long day. I'm off to bed."

"Whose bed?"

The last word was muffled as Lord Brackley kissed his wife soundly, silencing her. Happy to be ignored, Charlie took advantage of the distraction and slipped out of the room. She pressed her hands against her scorching cheeks as she reached the cooler air of the corridor.

When she reached the guest wing, where her bedchamber was situated, she paused. She stared at Anthony's door. A light still glimmered from the crack beneath it. He'd seemed unsettled when he'd gone to bed. Mostly likely, he agonized over the impending danger his mother would put herself in.

Lud. She couldn't leave him be, not when he needed comforting. She didn't give a damn what Lucy said to her later. She was going into that room to help Anthony in whatever way she could.

23

*G*ray jumped as the latch to the bedchamber rattled. He hadn't locked the door, thinking himself safe while in his sister's home. With the intrusion, he lunged from his position under the bed sheets, staring at the play of candlelight on the ceiling. He didn't reach halfway to his dirk on the writing desk before Charlie slipped into the room and shut the door.

Cursing, he lunged for the banyan that had been left for his use and wrapped it around his nude body. Her gaze raked down his front. Slowly, she returned her attention to his face. "Forgive me. I didn't mean to startle you."

She'd entered his bedchamber unannounced, which he thought would startle anyone. *Has she lost her bloody mind?* After double-checking that the sash tying his robe together was secure, he crossed to the door and reached for the latch. She stubbornly stood in the way.

"We're at my sister's house now. It isn't proper for you to be here."

Her gaze hardened, like flecks of aquamarine. "I'd think you'd know by now that I don't give a whit what is proper, not if it will interfere with us." She reached out and laid her hand on his silk-covered bicep. "I'm worried."

His resistance melted beneath her touch, and he gathered her close, laying his cheek atop her head. With her nearness, the knots in his shoulders and stomach started to loosen. "I'm worried, too," he confessed.

Truthfully, ever since retiring, he'd lain abed visualizing every horrible scenario they might find when they reached London. In the worst, not only was his mother dead, but the rest of his family had been hurt as well. With the rain lashing the side of the mansion, an audible reminder that he was trapped indoors, he'd never felt more helpless.

Breathing deep, he let Charlie's warmth sink into his bones. She smelled of the floral soap she must have used in her bath. His body stirred. He'd never wanted to kiss her more, but he knew that if he did, he wouldn't be able to stop. Instead, he drew away.

She didn't let him. Raising her hand, she cupped his newly shaven cheek and looked him in the eye. "We will save her. Together. Neither of us will abide for anything less."

The conviction in her voice raised a lump in his throat. He swallowed thickly. Turning his head, he pressed a kiss to her palm.

"You should leave," he whispered, his voice hoarse. He didn't want her to. When she was near, she put him at ease. No longer was he plagued by nightmarish scenarios. All he thought about—all he wanted to think about—was her.

All the more so when she ran her tongue across her lower lip. He burned, his gaze fastened to her mouth.

"Perhaps I should." Her voice was every bit as soft as his. "I don't much feel like doing what I ought to do right now."

Raising herself on tiptoe, she brushed her mouth over his. He was powerless to resist. Holding her head steady, he deepened the kiss. With his free hand, he pressed her against him. When she dipped her hand beneath the collar of his banyan, he trembled at the touch of her bare skin.

He broke the kiss, breathing heavily. "Charlie, you

must leave. If you stay... I don't know if I trust myself to stop."

She nibbled on her plump lower lip. "Do you want to stop?"

He swore under his breath. "No, I don't. That's the problem."

She twined her arms around his neck and pressed her body flush against his. It was torture. "I don't see a problem. I want this, too."

Lud! He wasn't nearly as honorable as he pretended to be. As he kissed her again, surrendering to the feel of her body, he placated himself with the knowledge that they would marry after this. He would offer her nothing less.

She moaned against his mouth as he ran his hands over her figure, learning every curve. Pleasure hummed through his veins, stoking his desire. He kissed her with all the pent-up passion he'd held in check since the moment they'd met. When she slipped her hands deeper beneath his banyan, he made no move to stop her.

Feverishly, he undid her buttons and untied the stays beneath. He moaned at the sensation of her smooth skin as he chased the fabric over her shoulders and down her arms. His breath caught as he revealed more of her beautiful body. She was a goddess, but he preferred when she had a challenging spark in her eye to when she looked uncertain.

Her cheeks were flushed with color. Her thick eyelashes veiled her eyes as she traced the hasty knot he'd tied in his sash. "Anthony?"

"Yes, love?"

"Do you think perhaps it's time to get into bed... beneath the sheets?"

He smiled, wondering how a woman so beautiful and brazen could suddenly be so shy. Cupping her chin, he kissed her gently. "You are beautiful, Charlie. Body and soul."

The pinkness in her cheeks deepened. "I never used to be. Growing up, I was the plainest girl to be found."

"You would still have been beautiful to me." He had to make her understand that the sparkle in her eye was her crowning jewel. Her laugh and smile brightened a room.

And her strength of character was remarkable—by now, any other woman would have showed weakness where Charlie displayed determination and compassion. No other woman could compare.

Since he could render none of that into words, he kissed her soundly. After a moment, he lifted her and carried her to the bed, relenting to her request. He would have years to enjoy the sight of her body. Decades.

As he shucked his banyan and slid into the bed next to her, he pulled the sheets over their heads. The candlelight cast an odd orange glow through the thin white fabric. Charlie licked her lips as he held himself over her.

"What are you doing?"

"I'm taking us on an adventure. Pretend we're someplace else, on a sandy beach in the Caribbean Isles."

The shyness in her expression melted into the shadows, leaving only a sly smile. There was the Charlie he knew and admired, the woman who made him burn. "Oh?"

"We're the only two people there. The water is lapping at your side." He ran his fingers over the left side of her figure, lightly trailing his touch over every sensitive hollow until she gasped and squirmed. He kissed her neck, tasting her skin. She felt incredible against him.

When he reached the swell of her breast, she moaned and arched backward. "It's hot in the Caribbean Isles."

He chuckled. "You make it that way, my dear. I've burned for you ever since we first kissed."

He continued his exploration of her body with lips and tongue, wanting to set her on fire the way she did him. It didn't take much to render her speechless.

By the time he reached her thighs, she quivered and moaned with need. He brought her to the brink with desire, her fingers digging into his shoulders, before he aligned their bodies once more. He kissed her, holding her close as he joined their bodies. From the moment he slid into her, he couldn't think of anything but the feel of her in his arms. Nothing mattered but that moment.

Desperate to reach that elusive pinnacle, he quickened his pace. Charlie's moans and the weight of her legs wrapped around him heightened his pleasure. As she threw her head back and shuddered around him, he followed her into bliss.

His arms trembled as reality returned. Out of breath, he fought to pull the sheets down around their shoulders once more. Before his arms could no longer hold his weight, he rolled onto his side next to her. He kept one hand on her stomach, possessive. This was the start of something much more between them.

Her mussed hair clung to her cheek as she smiled at him. "I think I saw the stars in the Caribbean Isles."

He grinned and kissed her shoulder. "I hope so. I worked hard to show them to you."

She cupped his cheek. "I had no idea it could be like this."

"Neither did I." He'd made love to women before, but none had made him feel the way Charlie did. He trailed his fingers over her stomach, reveling in the feel of her. "I imagine it will be even better when we're married. Morgan is a duke, and I'm certain he can arrange for a special license while we're in London. In case..."

Charlie tensed. She shot into a sitting position and clutched the sheet to her chest. When Gray imagined broaching the subject of marriage, he didn't expect the look on her face to be one of horror.

"Are you proposing to me?"

Charlie's breath caught as she spoke the words. Her heart hammered in the base of her throat. She'd thought she would have more time. And Anthony... He spoke as if it were a foregone conclusion. She wondered whether it was. Would she marry him?

He sat up but didn't bother to cling to the sheet. The candlelight illuminated the well-defined muscles of his chest beneath the mat of dark hair. Charlie battled the urge to touch him again, to feel his heart beat against her palm.

"I am... " He chose his words slowly, a furrow forming between his eyebrows.

"Why?"

That furrow deepened along with his frown. "Bloody hell, Charlie, we just—" He motioned to indicate the bed and the fact that they laid in it together with not a stitch on. "In case—"

Lucy had warned her about this, about his damnable honorable streak. His brothers carried it as well. In fact, Phil had once confessed to her that Morgan had proposed after a single kiss. Perhaps Charlie should be grateful she hadn't had to contend with *that*.

Lunging from the bed, Anthony retrieved the banyan from the floor and donned it hastily. He stood between her and her clothes.

Despite the intimacy they'd just shared, Charlie wasn't quite as bold to fetch her clothing. She clung to the cover of the bed sheet instead. "In case of what, Anthony?" She knew precisely what he meant to say, but she had to hear him say it first.

"In case I've gotten you in the family way."

If he'd wanted to avoid that, perhaps they never should have gone to bed together, after all.

No. She looked down and gathered her knees to her chest. She couldn't regret sharing her body with him. In fact, she refused. What she and Anthony had shared had been nothing short of magical. Even his honor couldn't erase that.

A sensible woman would accept the inevitability of marriage, but Charlie wanted adventure. She'd never planned to settle down so soon. Then again, she'd never planned to meet a man quite like Anthony, either. Surely he would never seek to prevent her from fulfilling her dream of adventure. He shared that dream. If he went on bended knee and professed his love to her...

But he hadn't. He spoke of children, of duty, not of love. Marrying simply because they ought to *would* be an anchor. She refused to do it to either of them.

Anthony lowered himself onto the foot of the bed in front of her. He reached out, taking her hand. "Charlie, surely you see the need to marry as well as I do."

The *need.* A chasm split her chest as if he'd used those words to stab her. A lump formed in her throat, but she swallowed it back. Perhaps she shouldn't expect him to talk of love, of how much he cherished and desired a life with her.

"I will not marry you because I must, Anthony. I'm not ready for domestic life. I want adventure."

His hand tightened on hers. "If you are with child—"

For heaven's sake, it had been mere minutes since they'd lain together. She couldn't possibly know or consider it so soon. She squeezed his hand before releasing it. "Freddie and Tristan have been married for over a year with no sign of babies. It isn't instantaneous. *If* it happens, then we will speak of it."

She didn't know what answer she'd give him if that happened. She met his gaze, pressing her lips together to keep from begging. *Tell me you love me.* Three small words might change her answer.

He didn't speak them. Instead, he ran a hand through his hair and sighed. He looked so vulnerable in that moment, but she hardened her heart. Her refusal was best for them both. He wouldn't thank her if he married her for the wrong reasons.

"Think on it," he said finally without meeting her gaze.

"My answer won't change." Her voice was thick with emotion. Swinging her legs around, she tried to keep her body behind the sheet as she rose. "I'm going to my room now. We have work to do tomorrow."

She cupped his cheek in her hand, but he still

refused to meet her gaze. The muscles in his jaw were as hard as rocks. As much as she ached to kiss him goodbye, she dropped her hand instead. She donned her clothes with haste.

When she reached the door, she glanced over her shoulder to find that he hadn't moved from that position. He looked as tortured now as when she'd entered. All she'd wanted was to offer him comfort—and take some for herself.

Oh, Anthony.

Her chest burned. As she departed, she tried not to think about whether she loved him or if she was making a mistake.

24

*G*ray spent the night staring at the ceiling and wondering how something so wonderful could have turned so awry. At one point, the candle guttered out. He must have fallen asleep after that, but when he woke, he was no more rested.

When the first rays of gray predawn light wafted through the window to illuminate the room, he rose and dressed. As he exited the room, he stopped short. Charlie, clad in her borrowed dress, halted with a hand still on the latch to her door, mere feet away. She looked as weary and worried as he did.

He battled the urge to take her into his arms and kiss her. The memory of her rejection erected an insurmountable wall between them. He couldn't look at her without remembering the horror on her face when he'd mentioned a special license. They'd formed a connection—or so he'd thought. He couldn't understand why she would have given her virginity to him if she didn't care for him.

For the adventure?

He tried to brush away the thought, but it persisted. That was the reason she'd cited for being unwilling to marry him. Lawks, he hadn't thought he was ready for marriage, either. But they'd shared themselves as man and wife, and he didn't want to cheapen their bond by pretending that it didn't mean something. She wasn't the same as the other women he'd lain with. He cared about her.

But seemingly, she didn't share that connection with him. Perhaps it was best that he focus on the much more important issue—his mother's safety.

Her eyebrows pulled together as she reached out to squeeze his arm. "Did you sleep at all?"

He pulled away.

The furrow in her forehead deepened, but she dropped her hand. She clenched it in front of her middle. Her posture stiffened.

He forced a smile. "I slept more than you, I imagine. I didn't hear your snores."

Her cheeks turned pink, and she averted her gaze.

"We were several rooms apart. I'm perfectly well rested."

Liar. He didn't have the courage to ask whether he h,if had . Instead, he murmured, "I hope so. We have much to do today. Let's hurry to breakfast. May I escort you?"

After the intimacy they'd shared, asking her that one simple question felt strange. She inclined her head but made no move to take his arm. He motioned for her to precede him instead.

At the staircase, they met Brackley, who was dressed for travel. It seemed he'd been serious when he said he meant to accompany them. A small weight lifted off of Gray's shoulders. If Brackley meant to come with them, they would meet with no more delays. The man was a marquess, with all the power and money that the title implied. They would reach London in time. They had to.

As they stopped within feet of one another at the landing, Gray inclined his head. "Brackley."

His brother-in-law returned the gesture but turned to Charlie. "Lucy warned me I might have to rouse you. I'm happy to see she was mistaken."

Charlie's answering smile was thin and wan. "This matter is too important for me to lay abed."

Brackley frowned. He looked between his two guests. "You seem different this morning. Is aught amiss?"

"My mother's life is in danger," Gray answered, his voice tight. "May we continue to the breakfast room?"

After gesturing to the staircase, Brackley fell into step with them. "Of course. Lucy will be down momentarily, and I mean to see us off as soon as possible. London is over a day's travel away by carriage, but if we go by horseback instead and ride hard, exchanging horses at every inn we pass, we might be able to reach the city this evening."

Neither Gray nor Charlie was the best of horsemen, but he nodded nonetheless. "Then that's what we'll do."

He didn't look to Charlie for confirmation. In fact, he was lucky that Brackley didn't underestimate her or Lucy. Perhaps he did love her, if he didn't try to coddle her.

Once again, his brother-in-law narrowed his eyes while glancing between them. He stopped in the center of the staircase. Gray would have walked past if Charlie hadn't also paused.

Brackley fixed them both under a penetrating stare. "Did something happen between you two last night?"

Gray clenched his teeth and managed not to glance at Charlie. Was she blushing? If she did, it would be impossible to keep their intimacy a secret.

Not that he wished to keep it a secret. No, he would rather shout it from the rooftops—by means of marriage, to which Charlie was violently opposed.

Squaring his shoulders, he answered, "No. Shall we continue?"

Brackley didn't budge. His frown deepened. "If there is friction between you, you'd best air it. Spy business is treacherous. You need to be able to trust your partner above all else."

Gray met Charlie's wide-eyed gaze for the briefest moment before he answered, "Charlie and I trust each other." His voice was edged with steel.

Lucy, clad in form-fitting breeches and a matching jacket, plodded down the stairs and stopped in her tracks as she reached the group. The air was thick with tension.

"Is something amiss?"

"Mother is in danger," Gray bit off. "Shall we hurry?"

"Of course." She insinuated herself beneath his arm and squeezed his middle. "We'll save her, Anthony."

He didn't know what he'd do if they couldn't.

* * *

FOAM GATHERED AROUND THE BIT ON THE HORSE'S mouth, a sure sign that they should have stopped on the outskirts of London to exchange beasts yet again. Twilight fell around them, the streetlamps not yet lit to provide better illumination. The result was a thin, dreary sort of fog that blanketed the cobblestones. Weary to the bone, Gray pulled his horse to a stop in front of the Tenwick townhouse.

Finally, they'd made it.

Although his legs felt like watered wine, he forced himself to dismount. A footman emerged from the townhouse. Gray locked his knees as he offered the man the reins. "We have to speak to Mother at once. Is she sitting down to supper?" He wouldn't feel at ease until he saw her with his own eyes.

"No, milord," the footman piped up. "I'm afraid she isn't at home."

Gray's legs threatened to give way. "Where is she?"

The young man tugged on his forelock as he avoided Gray's gaze. "I'm afraid she didn't leave her direction. She might be at the duke's residence with her sons."

Although he felt ready to collapse after a harried day, he dragged himself back into the saddle. They had to reach his brother's townhouse with all possible haste —if not, they might find themselves mere minutes too late.

25

*C*harlie didn't wait for the men to dismount and help her down. From the moment she pulled to a stop in front of the St. Gobain townhouse, she launched out of the saddle. On shaky knees, she crossed the cobblestones to the front door. No sooner did she raise her fist to knock than it was opened by a familiar face.

"Mr. O'Neill," she addressed the butler, a bit out of breath from the harrowing race through Mayfair to arrive here. "Is Lady Graylocke in?"

He looked surprised. "No, Miss Vale. I haven't seen her all day. I thought you weren't in London."

Still panting, Charlie waved her hand. "I wasn't. I just arrived. Is Morgan in his study?"

"I believe so... "

Charlie didn't wait for further invitation. She

knew the St. Gobain townhouse as well as she did the Tenwick townhouse, where she stayed while the family was in London. Gathering her skirt so she didn't trip over it, she stepped past Mr. O'Neill and raced through the house, up the steps to the second floor.

Morgan's office was smaller than his wife's secret inventing room a floor above, but he seemed perfectly at ease with it, as he and Tristan sat on opposite sides of the desk, discussing the sheaf of papers between them. Each had a page in their hands.

The moment the duke spotted her, he jumped to his feet. His pale-gray eyes pierced through her, but it seemed that they couldn't extract her inner secrets because he asked, "Charlie? What in the blazes are you doing in London? Shouldn't you be in France?"

She nodded, gulping for air. "Found Papa. No time to explain. Where is"—she panted—"your mother?"

The shock in Morgan's expression bled into a frown. "I don't know. She isn't here. What is this about?"

Anthony entered the doorway mere moments after her. "She's in grave danger. We must find her at once."

If the moment hadn't been so fraught with peril and worry over Lady Graylocke's fate, the twin looks of astonishment and delight on Morgan's and Tristan's faces would have been heartwarming. As it was, Charlie's heartbeat quickened at the thought of delaying due to prolonged greetings.

"Anthony?" Tristan shook his head. "How are you here? You never wrote to announce a visit. Did he?" He turned to look at Morgan, who confirmed his statement with a shake of the head.

"I haven't time to explain," Anthony answered, his voice clipped. He exchanged a look with Charlie before returning to his brothers. "The plot by Monsieur V—Mother is the target. If we don't get to her in time, the French might."

Fingering the white streak at his temple, the duke stepped from behind the desk. His demeanor transformed into the stiff, authoritative bearing of a general. "Mother? Why would she be a target?"

"I'll explain on the way. Just suffice it to say it's all part of Monsieur V's plan. Do we have any notion of where Mother might have gone? She's not at the house."

Tristan volunteered, "I had breakfast with her this morning. She said she was going to the modiste with Lady Cowper."

Anthony swore. "There must be dozens of modistes in London."

There were, but only one that Lady Graylocke had

taken Charlie to time after time. "I know where she'll be. There's a shop on Bond Street—"

Slipping his arm around to the small of her back, Anthony herded her from the room. "Lead us. We haven't the time to waste."

"Wait," Morgan called as he stepped into the corridor after them. "I'll call for the carriage to be brought round."

"We have horses waiting out front," Anthony said, voice clipped as he stepped past Lucy and Lord Brackley. "I'll meet you at the modiste."

Morgan caught his arm. "It won't take long. I don't know how far you've come, but I imagine your horses are tasked. We can't be seen in a panic, or the French will know and move up their timeline. We must play this smart. I imagine they'll have the house watched."

A tic started in Anthony's jaw as he ground his teeth.

Tristan squeezed between Anthony and Charlie. "I'll fetch Freddie from the house. She'll want to help." He met Charlie's gaze. "You said Bond Street?"

She nodded. "She'll know the place." Charlie had visited it with her sister more than once.

As Tristan disappeared down the steps, Morgan stared Anthony down, his eyes like chips of ice. From

Anthony's squared shoulders and tall posture, he didn't seem the least bit intimidated.

Softly and calmly, the duke said, "Let me take the lead on this, please. I know the French presence in London better than you. I can send out runners to monitor the situation and keep Mother safe once they find her. But I still don't see what this has to do with—"

"Then do so," Anthony cut him off. "I cannot stand here and do nothing."

Frankly, Charlie was surprised that he was able to appear so strong and rejuvenated when she felt watery inside. She clenched her teeth to keep from yawning. Her legs trembled from keeping her upright, but she refused to complain. Their mission was too important to postpone.

As Morgan slung an arm around his younger brother's shoulders and led him toward the stairs, he said, "I will. While we wait for the carriage to be readied, I'll need you to tell me as much as you can about the situation."

Charlie prayed their departure wouldn't be delayed too long.

* * *

THE SUN HADN'T YET SUNK BELOW THE HORIZON

as they pulled up to the curb in front of the Bond Street shop. Charlie chafed as Morgan forced them all to await the driver lowering the stairs for them to exit the carriage, for appearances. Charlie didn't give a damn about appearances, and neither, she wagered, did Anthony. She waited only long enough for the driver to open the door before she emerged first, taking his hand in order to keep her balance as she descended.

The others followed hot on her heels as they struck out for the door to the modiste. The middle-aged woman accompanied a stately woman out of the shop doors and used a key to lock up.

Charlie stopped short. "Where is Lady Graylocke?"

When the woman, Lady Cowper, pinned her beneath an arch stare, she belatedly curtsied. "Forgive me, my lady, I didn't mean to be rude."

Straight-backed, Morgan strode up next to her, prompting the older lady to bend in a curtsey.

"Forgive us," he said, his calm voice belying his stiff posture. "We must find my mother at once. She told us earlier she meant to accompany you to the modiste."

The plump seamstress dipped in a deeper curtsey.

"So she did, Your Grace. I'm afraid she was called away."

Charlie swallowed a lump in her throat. "Called away? Where?"

Anthony's hot form bracketed her back, lending her strength.

Lady Cowper answered, "I'm not certain, precisely. She received a message from the charity she sponsors. It seems they were having some kind of problem."

"Thank you," Morgan answered. "If you see her, please tell her to seek me out at home at once."

As they parted ways with the two women, Morgan directed them toward the carriage once more. They stepped out of earshot just in time for another carriage to pull to a stop. Tristan and Freddie exited.

Charlie's knees weakened at the sight of her sister's milk-pale oval face. Freddie had always been the person to set the world to rights whenever something went awry. Picking up her cobalt skirts, Freddie hurried to the group and embraced Charlie.

"Thank heavens you're all right," she whispered against Charlie's hair. "Is Momma..."

Charlie hastened to ease her sister's worry. Even though Freddie still acted mad at their father, Charlie knew that deep down she wanted to be reunited with him as much as Charlie had. "She's fine, and Papa, too. They'll be arriving any day."

As Freddie pulled away, her expression tight, she raised her voice and addressed Morgan. "What's happened? Tristan explained a little on the way. Evelyn is in danger?"

Morgan nodded, his expression solemn. "Part of the French plot, it seems."

"But why? She's unconnected to the spy network, except through you."

A flicker of unease and disbelief crossed Morgan's face.

Charlie answered for him. "Actually, she runs the network. Strickland is only the figurehead."

"So the information suggests," Morgan added. He didn't sound convinced. "I'll wait to have that confirmed by her."

"Don't you believe she's capable?" Charlie certainly did, and Anthony had accepted the information without question.

Morgan looked hesitant. "She's capable... but if it's true, why would she keep it from me?"

Perhaps because he had gone through such effort to keep his involvement with the spy network a secret from her. They both should have trusted each other more. But that wasn't the matter in question at the moment.

"She isn't here," Charlie informed them. "It seems she received a message with an emergency at a charity."

Freddie nodded immediately. "Yes, the Widows and Mothers Society. She's very involved in ensuring the welfare of widows and single mothers in the lower class."

Charlie had known that Lady Graylocke was involved with various charities, but she didn't know where to find them. "I've never been there."

"I have," Freddie answered. "You spent much of your time with Lucy before her marriage"—she nodded at Lucy—"but I often volunteered with Evelyn. I'll give the address to your driver. It sounds as though we don't have a moment to waste."

As she turned on her heel, her skirt swishing behind her, everyone bunched to follow. "Wait," Charlie said. Reflexively, she grabbed Anthony's hand, hoping that he at the very least would listen to her. "What if the message wasn't from the charity? It might have been a trap set by the French."

Morgan's mouth thinned. He looked grim. "We can't know for certain unless we can find the message boy. I'll try, but that will take time. In the meantime, we'll hope the message was genuine and we can find her with the charity."

As Morgan hailed a young groom from the boot of the coach and spoke with him in a low tone, Anthony squeezed Charlie's hand. "We'll find her there. We have to."

Despite the doubt wriggling in Charlie's stomach, she squeezed him back and tried to believe him.

CHARLIE'S STOMACH SHRANK THE MOMENT THE charity's secretary shook his head.

"Lady Graylocke was here—"

Thank heavens.

"But the matter was set to rights well over an hour ago. She left to make an impromptu visit to a friend who she believed could be persuaded to give employment to one of the young women who sought us out."

"Did she name this friend?" Morgan asked, his voice stiff.

"Mrs. Biddleford, I believe she said."

Charlie stepped back, frowning, as Morgan concluded his business with the man. Her sister, Lucy, and Anthony crowded around her, out of earshot of the two men. For a moment, Anthony looked as though he might bracket her shoulders with his palms, but he lowered his hands to his sides instead. A pity, for Charlie craved the comfort of his touch.

"Is something wrong?"

She tilted her face up to meet his. "Aside from the fact that your mother might be in imminent jeopardy?"

She hated herself the moment the words spouted from her lips. His expression clouded over with worry again.

Swallowing hard, she shook her head and wrapped her arms around her middle. "Why would Lady Graylocke seek out one of the most notorious gossips of the *ton*?" Mrs. Biddleford hadn't had a kind word to say about Freddie during the brief Season before Freddie fell in love and married Tristan. In fact, Charlie suspected that Mrs. Biddleford hadn't said anything kind about her, either.

"She often speaks with Theodosia about the women here. She and Hester—Miss Maize—volunteer here from time to time."

Freddie didn't seem the least bit concerned with the aberration, although, if she was to be believed, Lady Graylocke's association with those busybodies wasn't unusual. In fact, it was a frequent occurrence if

294 LEIGHANN DOBBS & HARMONY WILLIAMS

Freddie had been invited to use the women's Christian names.

"Then the fact that Mrs. Biddleford is Lord Strickland's aunt has no bearing on Lady Graylocke's choice of companion?"

Freddie shook her head, but Anthony didn't seem as convinced. Judging by his pensive frown, he shared her misgivings. Perhaps Charlie was seeing spies around every corner now, but this meeting could be more related to the spy network than to the charity.

They had no time to discuss the matter further. As Morgan approached, Lucy said, "Let's drive to Mrs. Biddleford's townhouse and find out."

This time, the journey took mere minutes. Mrs. Biddleford's home resided on a street crowded with houses pressed together, wall-to-wall. She had a neat pair of rosebushes flanking her door. When they knocked, a woman answered.

"I'm afraid Mrs. Biddleford is not at home."

Charlie's stomach dropped. Although she knew the answer, she had to ask, "Then I take it Lady Graylocke is not here, either?"

The old woman glanced from Charlie to Morgan. "Of course not."

Charlie pressed her lips together. They were too

late. Where could Lady Graylocke be—and what if they didn't find her in time?

The assassination might not be tonight.

Unfortunately, Morgan's earlier statement held too much merit. Charlie, Anthony, Lucy, and her husband had raced through London, causing a stir to anyone watching. Showing up on Morgan's doorstep in such a harried way might have led the French to suspect that they knew of the assassination plot and meant to stop it. Charlie worried that they might find her minutes too late.

Blinking back tears, Charlie glanced at Anthony. His face might have been carved from stone. His mouth was set in an unforgiving line.

Morgan kept his head. "Did Mrs. Biddleford and my mother leave together?"

"They did."

It wouldn't save her. If anything, it fulfilled the requirement for the assassination plot—among friends, in public.

"Do you know where they meant to go?"

The duke's voice was even, but his icy gaze did its work. The old woman wrung her skirt.

"T-t-to the theat-t-ter, Your Grace. I believe they meant to take in a play."

"Which theater? Which play?"

"I don't know. They didn't say."

The woman seemed close to tears. Freddie, her face scrunched with sympathy, squeezed to the front of the procession to pat the servant's arm. "Thank you. You've been very helpful."

But it might not have been enough. The moment the old woman shut the door, the family gathered around to discuss their options.

"We have to split up," Anthony said, his voice stern. "We'll each search one of the popular theaters. Wherever it is, it'll probably be where we have a standing box, so that leaves only four places to search."

They divided the four among themselves. Lucy and Alex took the carriage with Freddie and Tristan, each couple to search a different theater. Charlie and Anthony accompanied Morgan to His Majesty's Theater. Morgan left them there, saying, "I'll search the last. If you find Mother, bring her back to the house and keep her there."

The moment Anthony nodded in acknowledgement, Morgan shut the door and rapped on the roof of the coach. The carriage rattled away over the cobblestones.

Charlie took a single, calming breath then plunged into the crowd. Anthony remained on her heels, glaring at anyone who dared to look in their direction and clearing an easier path for them as they entered the lobby. He laid his hand on her back, guiding her toward the staircase leading to the private boxes on the upper floors. She balked.

"If we enter by the audience seats, we'll be able to see all the boxes. We'll find her faster." If she was there. If she wasn't, Charlie and Anthony could hurry to help Morgan at his allotted theater.

Unlike Charlie, Anthony didn't opt to shout over the babble and rustle of the crowd. He nodded and steered her along with the current of traffic into the swamp of seats in the theater.

Charlie pushed through the crowd as they thinned, claiming their seats. Once nearly to the stage, she and Anthony stopped. They each took a wing of the theater and peered at the scarlet-draped boxes above the audience. The rustle and fall of curtains behind the boxes distracted her, making it more difficult to tell how many people resided in each box and whether or not they matched Lady Graylocke's appearance. What she wouldn't do for a spyglass.

"I found her."

The breath gushed out of Charlie at Anthony's terse proclamation. She barely processed the words, and his pointing finger to a box on the second level, before he grabbed her hand and tugged her behind him on the way to the stairs. A small staircase, likely for those employed by the theater, rose from beside the stage to disappear on that level.

Grasping her skirts to keep from tripping over them, Charlie followed. She stumbled and almost fell into Anthony when he stopped suddenly. His grip tightened on her hand, a reflexive squeeze.

"Anthony, what—"

"Stay behind me, whatever you do."

As he started forward again, Charlie peered past him and caught the tail end of a shadow as a figure ducked up the stairs. *Could it be the assassin?* What if she and Anthony arrived too late?

Snatching her hand back, she said, "Hurry."

Her rapid heartbeat drowned out all other sound. As they reached the top of the stairs, she swallowed against a mouth as dry as sand, wondering where the figure had gone. As the rustle of opening curtains onstage wisped through the theater, the crowd quieted. The show was about to begin. No one aside from Anthony and Charlie lingered in the corridor.

They raced down the hall, Anthony counting the boxes aloud as he sought out the one where he'd seen his mother. As they reached it, he flung the curtain aside and barged in. Charlie marched in after him.

The box was empty, save for three women: Lady

Graylocke, Mrs. Biddleford, and Miss Maize. The two older ladies looked astounded at the intrusion. Lady Graylocke stood with a mixed expression of shock and delight. "Anthony?" She reached out her hands toward him.

Out of the corner of her eye, Charlie caught movement. A man, clad mostly in black, strode to the lip of the neighboring box. He lifted and cocked a pistol.

Charlie screamed Anthony's name. He bolted from the box the moment he saw the threat, rounding to intercept the assassin. He wouldn't reach the neighboring box in time. If Charlie didn't do something, Lady Graylocke was going to die in front of her eyes.

Out of sheer panic and desperation, Charlie threw herself in front of the woman who had come to be a second mother to her.

26

*T*he breath lodged in Gray's throat as he raced into the neighboring box. The swinging curtain buffeted his arm. As the assassin pulled the trigger, the report deafened him. His heart stopped beating as Charlie flung herself at Mother. Her momentum carried both women to the ground.

Heaven help him. It was bad enough his mother's life was in danger. He didn't know what he would he do if the woman he loved died.

His ears rang as the assassin fumbled for something in his pocket, ammunition or perhaps another loaded pistol. His instincts, honed from years of war, took over as he battled with the attacker. The traitor wasn't willing to submit without a fight.

Gray slammed him against the side of the box as his hearing cleared. The ring of the gunshot and rush of the blood in his ears was overpowered by the screams and shouts of the panicked mass of bodies in the theater. Breathing shallowly, he blocked out the sounds, focusing on the opponent in front of him.

It felt as though a lifetime passed before he rendered the man unconscious—a lifetime during which Charlie might be dying or already dead. The moment the man fell limp in his arms, Gray thrust him to the ground and ran to check on the two most important women in his life.

The two old biddies, friends of his mother, hovered over the women on the ground. *Are they still alive?* "Move," he commanded tersely. He didn't have the energy to curb his rudeness, not when every muscle in his body was attuned to the fate of the women on the ground. He'd dressed gunshot wounds in battle before. If he could only reach them...

Mother's friends stepped back, the curtain of their skirts revealing the women on the ground. Mother's mouth was tight, and she fought a grimace as she sat up. Charlie's face was flushed. With one curl clinging to the side of her mouth, she tilted her face back and asked, "Are we safe to stand?"

When he nodded, she held out her hands to him. If he helped her stand, he would pull her into his embrace.

She didn't want to marry him, and such a public display of affection would tie them together irrevocably. Unable to touch her in any meaningful way, he crouched and held her hands tight over his heart. "The devil take me, Charlie, why would you do that?"

She stiffened. "I saved your mother's life!"

He lifted her hands to his mouth, muffling his words as he breathed in her clammy skin. "Yes, and in so doing, you nearly stole mine."

He hadn't truly understood the depth of his feelings for her until her life was in jeopardy. He had once thought her wild and unlovable, but the opposite was true.

She was wild, yes, but she was also ladylike, fierce, and accomplished. Never in his life had he met a woman better suited to him, and he was certain he would never meet another woman like her again. Until he'd nearly lost her, he hadn't realized how much he needed her in his life—not only today, but every day thereafter.

He didn't want to marry her out of fear of having gotten her with child; he wanted to marry her so he would always come home to her. Now that their lives had intersected, he didn't know if he could live without her.

But she'd already refused his proposal once. She didn't want to marry him.

The thought muted the danger of the moment and disconnected him. He helped her to stand then aided his mother. When the taller of the older women—he didn't know which was Mrs. Biddleford—asked after the assassin, Gray numbly explained how he'd incapacitated the fellow but left him where he fell. Showing a great deal of mettle, the two biddies volunteered to watch him until help arrived.

It didn't take long. By the time he herded his mother toward the door as Charlie explained the situation, he spotted several figures moving against the current of the thinning crowd below. Morgan, easily identifiable due to the streak of white in his hair, led the figures.

The threat against his mother had been thwarted.

LATE THAT EVENING, A DISGRUNTLED FOOTMAN let Gray into Brackley's townhouse and led him to the study. He helped himself to the whiskey on the mantel as he awaited his sister. Despite knowing that his mother was now safe, the threat contained, and everyone in the network on high alert to prevent future attacks, Gray was no more at peace.

He couldn't stop thinking of Charlie. In a day or two, he'd have to sail down the Thames and back to his ship. Tomorrow, he had an appointment with an admiral in London to explain the situation with Lieutenant Stills. Through the course of that meeting, Gray would no doubt be commanded to resume his position at sea.

Although he would put in a request for special leave as soon as possible, he would have to leave Charlie behind. She was such a dynamic, lively woman, and he worried that someone else would notice her worth and she would fall in love while he was away. His stomach tied itself in knots around the smooth burn of whiskey.

"Anthony?"

He turned at his sister's sleepy voice. It was long past midnight. He must have woken her. She ran her fingers through her loose hair, arranging it over her wrapper as she stepped into the room.

"What are you doing here at this hour?"

"Other than to drink your husband's whiskey?" Gray tried for a smile, but it fell flat.

When he took one of the armchairs facing the hearth and the burning branch of candles there, Lucy took the seat opposite him. "Aren't you going to offer me some of your stolen whiskey?"

He smirked. "You're the lady of the house. Can't you pour your own?"

"It tastes sweeter when you do it."

Bollocks. He didn't correct her and smiled as he stood to fetch her a tumbler. He poured a scant finger into the bottom of the glass then offered it to her.

As she sipped, he asked, "Brackley... He's good to you?"

She looked him in the eye. "I wouldn't be married to him if he wasn't."

Gray swilled the amber liquid around his glass as he reclaimed his seat. "He has a history..."

"I know of his past. We love each other, Anthony."

Nodding, he took a sip. He savored the burn as he swallowed, buying himself time to think. In a soft voice, he admitted, "I love Charlie."

"I thought so. It's clear there's something between you."

He stared into his glass. "She won't marry me."

The silence between them lengthened. After swallowing the last of the alcohol, he set the tumbler on a low table between them. Lucy had her lips pressed together. She still stared at her glass.

"You know why," he guessed. From the way

Charlie had spoken of Lucy, he suspected Lucy was the one person in the world who best knew Charlie's mind, and that included Charlie's mother and sister.

Lucy rearranged a lock of her black hair. "She wants adventure. She doesn't want a husband and children to hold her back. Perhaps if you give her time... "

"I may not have time," he said, his voice tight. "I'm going back to the war in a couple days—"

He hated the look of disappointment that crossed her face. It was the same look Mother gave him whenever he left after a leave. The pleading in Lucy's voice was no better. "Must you?"

He swallowed hard and tried to keep his voice even. "Of course I must, Lucy. I'm a captain in the Royal Navy. I have a duty to my country and my crew."

"Fulfill your duty here. Our brothers do." She laughed softly, shaking her head. "Lud, it seems even Mother does."

"I have no talent for subterfuge. I'm a seaman. I wouldn't know who I was without my ship and the purpose it affords me."

She narrowed her eyes. "You knew who you were before you signed up to go to sea."

No, he hadn't. He'd been a boy, and one who acted out to get his father's attention. Gray had never known true discipline or true purpose until he'd joined the navy. He couldn't imagine leaving it. In fact, the concept made his stomach cramp. Imagining life in London, without the sea breeze in his hair or a new vista on the horizon, felt as though fetters clamped around his wrists and ankles.

Now he knew how Charlie felt about marriage. If only he could prove to her that she was wrong. He would never seek to hold her back. In fact, if he could, he'd bring her with him.

He stood, looking down at Lucy. "I'm going back to my ship, Lucy. I must."

She looked glum as she stared at her hands. She didn't say a word. That uncharacteristic silence, more than anything, told him how devastated she was to hear he was leaving again. Perhaps one day, she would understand. Perhaps Charlie could help her understand.

"I'm sorry to have woken you. Good night."

As he strode for the door, Lucy glanced up. "I think Charlie loves you, too."

His heart skipped a beat. He detoured to kiss the top of her head. "That was all I needed to hear."

Perhaps he had reason to hope, after all.

27

*C*harlie glowed with happiness as she slathered a piece of bread with marmalade. Across from her, Mama held Papa's hand and sipped her morning tea with a fond smile. Tristan, on Papa's other side, engaged him in a warm conversation about a card game they'd discovered they both enjoyed.

Freddie sat next to her husband, her hair and dress neat and her movements precise as she ate her breakfast. Although she appeared not to be paying much mind to the conversation, now and again the corners of her mouth would tip up in a fond smile.

For all the anger Freddie had harbored toward their father for his vices and his part in faking his death, she began to soften the moment Mama and Papa had arrived in London the day before.

Charlie had hoped she would. Freddie was a

gentle, kind soul, and keeping so angry must have made her miserable. Perhaps, now that the family was reunited at long last, they would be able to bridge the gap of years. Charlie smiled as she took a bite of her breakfast. She looked forward to being a family again, with the new addition of Tristan and the Graylockes.

As Lady Graylocke entered the room, she *tsk*ed. "You're all awake already! Why didn't you rouse me?" She pinned Charlie beneath a fond smile. "I thought you would opt to lie abed, for certain."

Charlie shrugged. "Perhaps I've spent too much time aboard a ship. I seem to rise with the mere whisper of sound." As much as she would have liked to lounge in bed as she used to, she didn't want to waste a moment with Mama and Papa. Perhaps the novelty of having Papa close by would wear off with time, but for now she meant to embrace every second.

Thinking of ships reminded her of one marked Graylocke absence. "Is Anthony still asleep?"

"He must have gone out," Lady Graylocke answered as she accepted a plate from a footman posted near the sideboard. "When I knocked, I found the room empty." She brought the plate, laden with eggs, bacon, and kippers, to the seat next to Charlie.

Charlie battled to hide her disappointment. Anthony had disappeared the day before, after informing them that he had to present himself to the nearest admiral. In the afternoon, Charlie had been distracted by Papa's arrival and hadn't noticed, but Anthony had only returned that evening, and he might mean to be out all day today, as well.

Perhaps he was avoiding her. Since she had turned down his proposal, he hadn't paid the least bit of romantic attention to her. Maybe she had made the wrong choice.

Lady Graylocke touched the back of Charlie's hand, her expression kind. "Have a bit of tea. That should perk you up."

Charlie thanked her and continued to eat with much less enthusiasm.

As she finished the last drop of her tea, a shadow blocked off the doorway to the corridor. Her breath caught as she lifted her gaze to meet Anthony's. Although he filled out any jacket to advantage, she had to admit that he looked particularly handsome when clad in a Royal Navy coat.

The sight reminded her of when they'd first met. Awareness of him permeated her body, but she tried valiantly to hide it. She tried to cover by taking a sip from her teacup, only to realize it was empty. Her cheeks warmed as she set the cup in its saucer once more.

Anthony turned from her to look at his mother. "I have news."

Lady Graylocke seemed to shrink. Her expression fell. "You're leaving."

"This afternoon." He stood straighter, squaring his shoulders. "This wasn't an official leave, Mother. I feared a reprimand for abandoning my ship in order to race to London to warn you. However, Strickland's missive saved me. As long as I return to my ship posthaste, I will see no punishment."

Charlie clasped her hands on her lap. Although relieved that he wouldn't face punishment or expulsion from the navy, she didn't want to part from him so soon. Not with things between them feeling so unfinished.

Unfortunately, Anthony looked so composed that she couldn't tell whether he was sorry to be parted from her. Perhaps he was relieved not to be near her. The thought made her even more sullen.

When he returned to sea, would he think of her at all? After all they'd been through, she wouldn't be able to forget him, even with the distraction of her family.

Her mouth a thin line, Lady Graylocke stood. "I'll send word to your brother and sister, if this is how it must be. Since we have so little time with you, let's make the most of it."

When Charlie stood as well, Anthony's attention returned to her, his gaze unreadable. What she wouldn't give for one more moment alone with him before he left.

Unfortunately, it was not to be.

THE ENTIRE FAMILY ACCOMPANIED ANTHONY TO the docks. As the procession of carriages pulled to a stop, Freddie mumbled a complaint about the stink. To Charlie, the ripe, fishy smell seemed more like one of adventure. She'd never sailed along the Thames to the sea, and she contemplated what Anthony would think about while he did.

Freddie clasped a perfumed handkerchief over her nose and mouth. When she offered one to her sister, Charlie declined.

Although Felicia and Gideon currently remained at Tenwick Abbey with Phil and the baby, Charlie didn't trust the handkerchief not to contain a splash of one of Felicia's special love perfumes. The only man whose love she wanted was about to step onto a boat and sail away.

After everyone disembarked from the string of three carriages, Anthony said his individual goodbyes.

He shook hands with his brothers and embraced his mother and sister. Once he'd said a few words and exchanged some tearful farewells, he reached Charlie last.

She blinked back tears, trying to remain composed. This was goodbye. Would he kiss her hand as he had Freddie's, like there was nothing lingering between them?

When he reached for her hand, she gave it to him gladly, wishing that she hadn't worn gloves. He didn't bow over it or kiss it. Instead, he held it in both of his as his gaze caressed every curve of her face. It lingered on her mouth before he made eye contact once more. "May I speak with you alone a moment?"

Charlie nodded, though what privacy they could find with their families staring at them in the middle of a crowded dock, she didn't know. He led her to one end of the carriages, off the path where pedestrians passed without giving them a spare thought. Although her back was to her family, she felt their rapt gazes acutely.

"This is goodbye." She whispered to disguise the lump of tears in her throat.

"For now." He caressed her hand with his thumb. "I've put in a request for a longer furlough. Once it's approved, I hope to return for a merrier occasion than the mad dash we made across England."

She managed a thin smile but didn't know what to say.

"I have something for you, a token I pray you'll accept." Dipping his hand into his pocket, he removed a round box that fit in his palm. The top was carved and painted with a seaside landscape. Turning over her hand, he placed the box in her palm.

"What is this?" she asked as she caressed the lid with her thumb.

He smiled and answered, "Adventure."

When she opened the lid, she found a ring. A large, oval sapphire surrounded by a spray of tiny diamonds. Anthony sank down onto one knee and took her free hand.

"My dear, I'd think you would know by now that I would never seek to make you unhappy or make you feel tethered. You are as wild at heart as I am, and it is one of the things I love best about you."

Charlie swallowed hard. She blinked away tears as she admired the ring on its velvet bed. "You love me?"

"More than anything. I can't fathom a life without you, Charlie. I pray that in some corner of your heart you feel the same."

She nodded, for the moment unable to speak. "I

do. The only reason I didn't accept before was because I didn't want you to regret it. I want you to marry me because you want to, not because you have to."

His hand tightened on hers. A sheen glistened in his eyes as he smiled. "I want to. Darling, you have no idea how much. Will you make me the happiest of men and become my wife?"

"It would be my pleasure."

Charlie's head spun in the chaos of embraces and congratulations after he laid the ring on her finger. In the wake of their families' enthusiasm, he found his way back to her and bid her adieu.

As he boarded the vessel to transport him closer to his command and the frightening war, Charlie blew him a kiss. He had to leave, but she soothed herself with the knowledge that he would soon return.

And when he did, the best adventure of their lives would begin.

EPILOGUE

*L*ady Evelyn Graylocke smoothed her mauve skirts and looked into the curious faces of her family. My, how it had grown in these past two years.

All of her children had found happiness in spouses she was overjoyed to welcome into the family. Charlie, in particular, had been like a daughter to her ever since Freddie had married Tristan. That she and Anthony had found their way to each other threatened to turn Evelyn into a watering pot once more.

She blinked back a wave of tears as she turned her attention to Phil, newly arrived from the country with her son, Oliver, Evelyn's first grandchild, the future Duke of Tenwick, in her arms. It seemed fitting to give her family the explanation she owed them while the next generation was present.

Morgan seemed relieved to be reunited with his wife once more. The fond look in his eyes as he looked at Phil brought an ache to Evelyn's chest. She remembered when his father had looked at her that way, while she held Morgan. She took a deep, steadying breath as she sought out a safer avenue of thought.

The Vales were present, winged by both their daughters. Mr. Vale seemed to have accepted Tristan as his son-in-law wholeheartedly, for which Evelyn was glad. Gideon stood in the back corner next to his wife. He seemed agitated as she whispered something in his ear. Whatever it was, it appeared shortsighted when she elbowed him in the side. He winced and rubbed the spot. When he dropped a kiss on the top of her head, her displeasure dissolved into a smile. She teased him with a whispered quip that made him smile.

Jared, standing off to the side, heard the topic of the whispered exchange and shot them both a bizarre look. Evelyn contained a smile behind her hand. That poor boy looked haggard, and she wouldn't be able to ease his burden anytime soon.

Although Monsieur V and his spy network were no more, the war with Napoleon was far from over. Nevertheless, Evelyn vowed to redouble her efforts to find the woman Jared pined over and their son. The woman was skilled, but no one could hide from the Commander of Crown Spies. Evelyn would find her.

From the chair next to hers, Lord Strickland coughed into his fist. He raised one eyebrow toward his bald pate, as if reminding her of why he'd come to support her. Evelyn straightened as her extended family turned their attentions to her.

"I know it has come as something of a shock to you to learn that I command the Crown spies, especially considering that you are all a part of my network."

"A shock?" Morgan tightened his arm around his wife's shoulders and sat straighter on the settee. "I'm Strickland's second-in-command! I understand the necessity of keeping it a secret from the enemy, but why wouldn't you tell your own son?"

Raising her eyebrows with bemusement, Evelyn pointed out, "I'm your mother, and you never thought to tell me about *your* involvement."

He frowned. "That's... different. You knew of my involvement, whereas I didn't have the faintest inkling of yours. I was trying to protect you from worrying."

Evelyn smirked. "I know, dear. But I've been doing this since before you were born. I'll worry anyway—it's a mother's prerogative."

Sitting next to Tristan and holding his hand, Freddie frowned. "Did you know about the French spies the entire time? If so, why would you invite Harker into your home?"

A shadow overcame the Vales as they relived a troublesome time in the past. Evelyn wanted to comfort them, but now wasn't the time. Mr. and Mrs. Vale were finally reunited, and their daughters had each fallen in love with one of Evelyn's sons. Despite the hardships in the past, everything had worked out to advantage.

"I knew," Evelyn confessed. "In fact, I tempted him with the code book on purpose. I didn't know that he would attempt to use Freddie to do his bidding, nor did I expect it to end with such bloodshed. I asked him so I could bring Louisa"—she nodded at Mrs. Vale—"to the house, in the hopes of using her considerable skill on other future assignments. She's been doing odd jobs for me, things that need a delicate touch, ever since Harker's death. And of course, keeping an eye on Lucy when Monsieur V targeted her until I knew Alex was partnering her."

Her son-in-law inclined his head.

Tristan raised an eyebrow and joked, "You don't think I have a delicate touch?"

Freddie blushed and smacked him on the arm with her free hand.

Evelyn smiled. She turned to Phil and Morgan. "I

admit, I arranged for you to go out on field assignment and had you cross paths with Phil because I hoped you would be smart enough to recruit an inventor of her caliber into the network."

Phil smirked, the expression making her seem mischievous. She adjusted her hold on her son to turn and wink at Morgan. "It turns out he was even smarter than anticipated."

Evelyn laughed. "Yes, I must admit I like having you for a daughter-in-law even more than I like having your inventions on hand to aid in our efforts."

From the back of the room, her youngest son sighed. "Please tell me you didn't arrange for Felicia to join us, too."

His wife straightened and glared up at him. "Why not? I'm a delight!"

"You cannot fathom how many times I ranted about you to Mother while you were set on belittling my work."

"I was not belittling." Felicia paused for one serene moment before she added, "I was correcting."

He tucked her into his side. "I am the botanist. You are the chemist."

Evelyn held up her hands to stall the playful bickering. "I did send Morgan to recruit Felicia because of all you'd told me about her. You must admit, you and she work brilliantly together and help us immensely."

"See?" Felicia said, drawing out the word as she tipped her head up to nettle her husband. "A delight."

Amused, Morgan shook his head. "You seem keen on sending me out as your personal errand boy, despite us never actually speaking on the subject. Wouldn't it have been easier to confess your part in this, rather than giving me direction through Strickland?"

"Perhaps." Evelyn shrugged. "I was waiting for you to tell me about your involvement." She raised her eyebrows. "I planned to tell you at the same time."

His cheeks turned pink. *Lud.* She hadn't been able to do that since he was a boy. She smiled to see him so contrite.

He coughed into his fist. "I take it, then, that it was no accident that Lady Belhaven sought me out to ask after Rocky's help in her greenhouse?"

"Goodness me, no. That poor woman would have worked herself to the bone if I hadn't intervened and told her about our broken orangery. She asked you to do me a favor, though I am glad it taught her to keep a botanist on staff, even if I'd never let her have our Rocky for so long." She smiled, a bit saddened that Rocky and her husband, Catt, were out on assignment at the moment and hadn't been privy to this explanation. The young woman had been a part of their household for years, and Evelyn was very fond of her. After a moment's pause, she added, "I convinced Lady Belhaven to throw one last masquerade, as well. She was famous for them when she was younger, I'll have you know."

Lucy smiled, a gleam in her eye. "It was a masquerade to remember. You knew I was pursuing Monsieur V all along? Why didn't you try to stop me?"

Evelyn raised her eyebrows and looked from Lucy to her eldest son. "I always disagreed with Morgan's decision not to involve you like he did your brothers. You, my dear, have the passion and mettle for spy work, and I've always known it. So when I learned that you were involved, I concealed it from your brother but arranged for Mrs. Vale to keep an eye on you." She nodded to Charlie, on the other end of the string of Vales—though she wouldn't be a Vale for much longer. Evelyn couldn't help but smile at the reminder of the impending wedding. "I would have liked to help your assignment better than I did. Such a shame about Madame Renault."

Charlie frowned. Her hand hovered near the edge of her bodice before she balled it in her lap. "You could have told me we had arranged to stay with a fellow spy.

You could have trusted me to keep your purpose in the spy network a secret."

Guilt churned in Evelyn's stomach. Considering the way the matter had come to light, perhaps she would have done better to trust them with the knowledge to begin with.

Before she could say a word, Strickland leaned forward. "We kept this a secret for good reason. We didn't want your mother to meet her end in the same way as your father did."

Her children exchanged glances. Tristan was the first to speak up. "Father was a spy?"

"The commander," Strickland confirmed. "I was his assistant for many years, until his involvement ultimately led to his death. From that moment, your mother and I made a decision that I should the figurehead while she took true command. That way, if anyone should think to disrupt the network, as they so clearly did, they would target the wrong person."

Somehow, the enemy had learned of her involvement in any case. She didn't know how, but she prayed the information had been contained to those Monsieur V trusted the most. Everyone in this room had a formidable task ahead of them still, to discover every last French spy privy to that information and lead them to capture.

As if to punctuate her thoughts, Strickland added, "We must all keep this a secret, for Evelyn's safety."

Heads nodded around the room as everyone agreed, their faces set in determination. Morgan, the natural leader of them all, laid a hand over his son's legs as if to bolster his resolve. "Without question." He caught Evelyn's gaze and held it, his eyes every bit as piercing as his father's. "Now that we have all our secrets out in the open, we'll be able to work together that much more efficiently. For the next generation, we will end this war and keep the people of Britain safe."

Evelyn let her gaze drop to Oliver with a smile. Although a pang of grief struck her that her husband wasn't with them to see his grandson grow and thrive, her chest warmed with love.

Oliver was a reminder of why they all, including Anthony, put their lives on the line in order to protect their country. They did it for love.

And they always would.

****

Have you read the rest of the Scandals and Spies series?

Kissing the Enemy (Book 1)
Deceiving the Duke (Book 2)
Tempting The Rival (Book 3)
Charming The Spy (Book 4)
Pursuing the Traitor (Book 5)

Sign up for Leighann's VIP reader list and get her
books at the lowest discount price:
http://www.leighanndobbs.com/newsletter-historical-
romances

If you want to receive a text message on your cell
phone for new releases, text ROMANCE to 88202
(sorry, this only works for US cell phones!)

Join Leighann's private Facebook group and get the
inside scoop on all her books:

HTTPS://WWW.FACEBOOK.COM/GROUPS/LDOBBSREA
ders/

ALSO BY LEIGHANN DOBBS

Regency Romance

* * *

Scandals and Spies Series:

Kissing The Enemy

Deceiving the Duke

Tempting the Rival

Charming the Spy

The Unexpected Series:

An Unexpected Proposal

An Unexpected Passion

Dobbs Fancytales:

Dobbs Fancytales Boxed Set Collection

———

Western Historical Romance

***

Goldwater Creek Mail Order Brides:

Faith

American Mail Order Brides Series:

Chevonne: Bride of Oklahoma

Contemporary Romance

***

Reluctant Romance

***

Sweetrock Sweet and Spicy Cowboy Romance

Some Like It Hot

Too Close For Comfort

Magical Romance with a Touch of Mystery

***

Something Magical

Cozy Mysteries

Silver Hollow

Paranormal Cozy Mystery

* * *

A Spell Of Trouble

Mystic Notch

Cat Cozy Mystery Series

* * *

Ghostly Paws

A Spirited Tail

A Mew To A Kill

Paws and Effect

Probable Paws

Blackmoore Sisters

Cozy Mystery Series

* * *

Dead Wrong

Dead & Buried

Dead Tide

Buried Secrets

Deadly Intentions

A Grave Mistake

Spell Found

Mooseamuck Island Cozy Mystery Series

* * *

A Zen For Murder

A Crabby Killer

A Treacherous Treasure

Lexy Baker Cozy Mystery Series

* * *

Lexy Baker Cozy Mystery Series Boxed Set Vol 1 (Books 1-4)

Or buy the books separately:

Killer Cupcakes

Dying For Danish

Murder, Money and Marzipan

3 Bodies and a Biscotti

Brownies, Bodies & Bad Guys

Bake, Battle & Roll

Wedded Blintz

Scones, Skulls & Scams

Ice Cream Murder

Mummified Meringues

Brutal Brulee (Novella)

No Scone Unturned

Contemporary Romance

***

Reluctant Romance

***

Sweetrock Sweet and Spicy Cowboy Romance

Some Like It Hot

Too Close For Comfort

ROMANTIC SUSPENSE

WRITING AS LEE ANNE JONES:

***

The Rockford Security Series:

ABOUT LEIGHANN DOBBS

USA Today Bestselling author Leighann Dobbs has had a passion for reading since she was old enough to hold a book, but she didn't put pen to paper until much later in life. After a twenty-year career as a software engineer with a few side trips into selling antiques and making jewelry, she realized you can't make a living reading books, so she tried her hand at writing them and discovered she had a passion for that, too! She lives in New Hampshire with her husband, Bruce, their trusty Chihuahua mix, Mojo, and beautiful rescue cat, Kitty.

Find out about her latest books and how to get discounts on them by signing up at:
http://www.leighanndobbs.com/newsletter-historical-romances

If you want to receive a text message alert on your cell

phone for new releases, text ROMANCE to 88202 (sorry, this only works for US cell phones!)

Connect with Leighann on Facebook

https://www.facebook.com/leighanndobbshistoric
alromance/

ABOUT HARMONY WILLIAMS

If Harmony Williams ever tried her hand at being a chemist, she would probably wind up blowing something up like Giddy almost did. Instead, she lives an explosion-free life in the middle of the Canadian countryside with her enormous lapdog, Edgar. In her spare time, she likes to sip tea, read too many books (if such a thing is possible) and dream up funny new ways for characters to fall in love in Regency England. Join her newsletter at www.harmonywilliams.com/newsletter and get a free novella!

38008013R00191

Made in the USA
San Bernardino, CA
05 June 2019